COWBOY

BLACK OPS MMA BOOK 4

D.M. DAVIS

Copyright © 2022 D.M. DAVIS

COWBOY
Black Ops MMA Series by D.M. DAVIS

ISBN: 978-1-7354490-9-8

Published by D.M. DAVIS

www.dmckdavis.com
Cover Design by D.M. DAVIS
Cover Photo by Michelle Lancaster
Cover Model Mark Robinson @healthmanmark
Editing by Tamara Mataya
Proofreading by Mountains Wanted Publishing & Indie Author Services
Formatting by Champagne Book Design

This book is a work of fiction. Names, characters, places, and incidents are either the product of the author's imagination or are used fictitiously.

The octagonal competition mat and fenced-in design are registered trademarks and/or trade dress of Zuffa, LLC.

This story contains mature themes, strong language, and sexual situations. It is intended for adult readers. Some scenes may have triggers.

ABOUT THE BOOK

COWBOY is an angsty, heart twisting, second chance, contemporary sports romance and Book Four in the *Black Ops MMA* series.

I was young and naïve when I met my other half.
I was a good guy, full of hopes and dreams.
Falling head over heels for my Songbird.
She stole my breath.
Rocked my world.

Then she trampled my heart the day she disappeared, ghosted me. Her absence haunted me, tainted my future, destroyed my dreams, left me fighting for steady ground.

Years later, she shows up where I least expect, belonging to those who can make or break my MMA career, or worse, get me disowned from my family by choice.
She acts like I don't exist, like she doesn't know me, like she doesn't remember the love we shared.
I'm good with that.
I have every intention of leaving her in my past where she belongs.
And yet... I can't stop the wanting, the craving, the claiming.

Nothing could have prepared me for the truth of why she left, what happened afterwards, or the shattering journey that brought her back to me.

Some secrets are worse than the perceived truth.

NOTE TO READER

Dear Reader,

First off, thank you for picking **COWBOY** as your next read. I'm deeply grateful and appreciative, and for that reason I want to advise:

For maximum enjoyment, I suggest the *Black Ops MMA* Series be read in order to fully experience the world and the yummy alphas (and their amazing women) who inhabit it. Though each book is a standalone, they are integrated with subplots that carry through Books 1-4.

Please start with NO MERCY, then ROWDY, and CAPTAIN, before diving into **COWBOY**.

Content Warning: COWBOY deals with sensitive topics such as sexual assault and stalking that could be triggering for some.

XOXO,
Dana
(D.M. DAVIS)

PLAYLIST

Burn Fast by Bryce Fox

Happiest Year by Jaymes Young

Save Your Tears by The Weeknd

Lifeline by We Three

Latch by Sam Smith

In Between by J.J. Pfeifer featuring Grace Meredith

What Hurts The Most by Aaron Lewis

What Are You Listening To by Chris Stapleton

Fingers Crossed by Lauren Spencer-Smith

Party of One by Brandi Carlile featuring Sam Smith

You and I by Lady Gaga

Ocean by Lady A

The Bones by Maren Morris

Closer (Vol.1 Ch.1) by victoria

Blinding Lights by The Weeknd

You and Me by Lighthouse

Fix You by Canyon City

Ready by Sam Fischer

The Good Ones by Gabby Barrett

We'll Figure It Out by Smithfield

Starting over by Chris Stapleton

Shade by Maren Morris

Always Been You by Shawn Mendes

The Bones by Maren Morris and Hozier

Best Part of Me by Ed Sheeran Featuring Yebba

DEDICATION

For the readers who love my Black Ops alphas.

COWBOY

BLACK OPS MMA BOOK 4

CHAPTER 1

"**B**OSS, SHE'S READY." LEO, MY GENERAL MANAGER, motions to the stage.

I grumble something unintelligible and continue to stock the bar. We'll be open in a few hours. I don't have time to give to the heartbreaker on the stage.

She looks innocent enough. Actually, she looks downright petrified, nothing like the girl I fell for, who was fearless, full of life, and strikingly beautiful. This version of Taylor is still beautiful, if not on the too-skinny side of healthy, her nervous hands that used to touch me in the hungriest of ways far too fragile. But it's the fear in her eyes that's a hot poker to the chest and keeps my eyes glued to the task at hand: restocking the bar.

Mel's Bar was bequeathed to me by the former owner, along with substantial savings, which has allowed me to keep the doors open with the existing employees—including myself—and renovate the areas in desperate need of attention. Mel took a shine to me when I started working here a few years ago, right after Cap brought me to Vegas from California. I had no idea Mel was sick and was looking for someone to leave the place to. I guess I fit the bill. He was a great guy, down to earth, *give you the shirt off his back* kind of guy, *give you a bar because*—shit I don't know why—kinda guy. I guess I looked like I needed something steady to rely upon. To fall back on if I fucked up MMA as I did football.

When her sweet, smoky voice fills the air, I grip the counter, squeezing my eyes tight, focusing on breathing to find my center she so easily knocked off-kilter with one damn note, one strum of her guitar. It takes everything I have to stay planted with my back to her.

Ignore her.

Pretend she doesn't exist, just like she's been doing to you since Rowdy's wedding.

I'm a good guy. I *was* a good guy before I met *her*. The highest-ranking high school QB in the nation for my graduating class, my life was set, my future was strong, promising, mapped out. Then it all went to shit. I lost it all: the college scholarship, NFL draft prospects, fame, admiration, and the respect of my friends and family.

In what felt like the blink of an eye, I fell for a golden-haired goddess. I was blazingly happy, hopeful, and content beyond words.

Then I lost her, went off the deep end, let everyone down when I shattered my reputation, future, and my throwing arm into a million unrecognizable, useless pieces.

I didn't have a backup plan, not an intentional one. I fell into mixed martial arts as a kid. My mom enrolled me for her sanity, but I learned structure, discipline, patience, dedication, and respect. It made me stronger mentally and physically. It was the foundation of my football career.

An MMA career wasn't the goal, until it was. And as much as I want to succeed, I've learned my lesson. *Have a backup plan and don't, under any circumstances, fall in love—again.*

When breathing and clenching my jaw so tight I fear I might pop a tendon don't work, I leave the rest of the restocking to Jake the moment he comes in. "I'll be in my office," I tell Leo as I pass, not giving the songstress a single glance nor acknowledgment.

She wants to act like she doesn't know me? Yeah, well, same.

How bad will Rowdy whoop my ass if I tell his baby sister she can't work here? I sigh into the office door after closing it, banging my head against it to knock some sense into me and the memories of her out.

He'll kick your ass back to Texas if he finds out you slept with her.

"Fuck. Fuck. Fuck." I lift my fist to hammer the door but stop at the last second. "Get a grip."

I have to act like I don't know her.

If I didn't know Rowdy's sister, I'd absolutely hire her. A handful of notes and I already know she'll draw in the male customers—and more male customers draw in the babes. It's a win-win. Except, I *do* know Taylor, and hiring her is the last thing I should do.

It's also incredibly suspicious if I don't.

I'm screwed in every way possible except the pleasurable ways. All the ways she loved me, until she didn't.

Can you die from embarrassment? I barely make it to the chorus before Landry rounds the bar and skulks across the room, disappearing down the hall to the bathrooms, storage room, employee breakroom, and office. The only reason I know what's down the hall is Leo showed me around when I entered through the back door. Mel's Bar isn't even open yet.

Landry didn't glance my way. Not once. Not a nod, a tip of his non-existent hat, no hello, no *fuck you very much*. Nothing. He gave me nothing. No recognition. No acknowledgment I was even in the same room with him, much less the same city.

It hurts, but I don't blame him. I haven't treated him any better since I arrived from Texas—really since Rowdy's wedding. I started this silent pretend-we-don't-know-each-other agreement. He's just following my lead. He's a nice guy like that—usually. I deserve every dirty look, scowl,

3

nasty word he doesn't say, but I feel all the same on the rare occasion his gaze does land on me.

Him being good at hiding his hateful feelings doesn't mean they aren't there.

I keep singing. I won't let them—*him*—see me break. I need this job—it's the best opportunity I've got, even if the connection is through my brother and tenuous. I pour my heart into the song I picked for Landry, not even knowing he'd be here to hear it. It allows me to say things I can never speak. I ask what song is he listening to. Does he play it on repeat? Does he think of me when a love song or broken-heart song plays? Does he ache for me? Does he miss me?

He couldn't possibly hurt as much as I do, or he'd show it on his face, in his mannerisms. The man I knew never would have let me go a minute without knowing I was on his mind—in his heart.

Though, I am the one who broke us. I'm to blame. I let him down. Let myself down. Let my whole family down.

As I play the last chord, the thought of asking Cap or Cameron for money springs to mind for the millionth time. They'd let me live off them. I refuse to touch my trust fund—a fund set up by my parents, who... I can't even go there.

I could pick up more hours at Cher's bakery to tide me over, but I love to sing and put my passion on the back burner for college to get a degree that benefited my family's business. Corporate law is far more stable than becoming a dive-bar singer. But I need to rely on myself. Learn to the walk the line and know I can make it on my own. As it is, the two weeks it took me to get to Vegas certainly don't bode well for proving I'm self-sufficient while not compromising my dreams.

Leo and the few employees in the room clap as I smile and set my guitar in its case. I thank whoever is listening for saving my guitar when everything else was taken.

It has to mean something. Doesn't it?

"Taylor, that was great." Leo stands at the edge of the stage stairs, a genuine smile softening his striking features. He offers his hand. "Come meet the boss."

"Thanks." I take his assistance and my momma's advice reminding me to never turn down a courteous gesture from a well-mannered gentleman. Encouragement is needed before good manners become extinct.

Yes, Momma.

How well-mannered is it for you to have babies from another man and not tell him or your kids?

Silence.

Yeah, she never responds when I get spiteful, which is more and more these days.

"You can leave your case here." Leo points to a table near the stage.

I grip it tighter. "I'd rather keep it with me if it's all the same." I nearly lost my girl when everything was stolen, not taking a chance when I have a choice. I don't know these people. They don't care about me.

He laughs at my possessiveness. "Sure. It just seems heavy. No worries." He leads me down the same hall Landry took. "This is just a formality. I pretty much handle the talent, but he signs the paychecks. It's good you meet."

"Of course." Why wouldn't I meet the boss?

He glances at me a second longer before knocking.

A grunt comes from the other side. "It's open."

"Boss—" Leo opens the door, blocking my view, "—thought you should meet the new talent."

Shuffling from inside has me peering over Leo's shoulder into the hazel eyes of my first love—my only love.

Landry's scowl deepens when he sees *I'm* the talent, like he didn't just hear me singing five minutes ago. But... he's the boss?

Guess there's no chance he and the *real* boss are sharing an office...

Leo turns to let me pass. "I'll leave you two to get acquainted." He disappears, closing the door behind him.

Yeah, we're far beyond *acquainted.* "I thought you were the bartender."

"Used to be. Sometimes still am. Officially I'm the owner and your boss." He sits, pointing at one of the chairs in front of his desk, barely looking at me.

"Does that mean I have the job?" I can only hope it's this easy.

He frowns, shuffling papers around, looking for something, then slides a piece of paper my way, sighs and sits back. "Fill that out. You can open for our headliner on Friday. Seven sharp. Twenty-minute set. If that works out, we'll talk about adding more nights."

"Twenty minutes?" I can't live on what he'll pay me for only twenty minutes *maybe* a few nights a week.

His eyes narrow, not a hint of warmth. "Not enough? Too much? What do you need, Taylor? Spit it out so I can get back to work."

Wow. His assessing gaze doesn't give anything away. There's no warmth in his hazel eyes, no hint of knowing me or having ever given a shit about me. I don't recognize the hard man before me. What happened to the sweet guy I fell for all those years ago? Did I do this to him? No, can't be. It's been too many years for him to still think of me like that and feel anything. Yet… I still think of him and feel…

And he just asked me what I need.

I swallow my pride and push through my uncertainty. "I need more hours."

He nods, biting the end of a pen.

I remember the sounds that mouth could pull from me. I've never been kissed like he kissed me, like heaven and forever were in my mouth, along my skin and—

"I need a certified bartender. Any chance you're one of those?"

"Uh, no."

His scowl deepens. At this rate, he'll need help lifting those brows of his if he ever attempts to smile.

"Barback? Waitress?"

"My background is more around corporate law and bookkeeping."

His brows shoot up this time, and without any assistance. "I have a lawyer, and the books…" He stands, making his way to the door. "I can give you a few shifts as a server, but…" He grips the knob but stops, glaring at the door. "If you're a lawyer, I don't know why you're here. You could make far more money practically anywhere else."

Yeah, but I wouldn't get to see you or a chance to sing and see if I can make a living at something I love instead of family obligation. I never wanted to be a lawyer. Plus, I still have to pass the bar, so...

I stand. He's obviously done with me. "Serving would be great. I finish at the bakery usually around two, so I'm free any time after that."

He crosses his arms over his formidable chest. A chest much broader than it was when I knew what it felt like to be held by him. Safe. Secure. Wanted. "We don't open till five."

"Okay."

He glares at me longer than feels comfortable. He's blocking the door, so he's not waiting on me to leave, unless he expects me to squeeze by him.

"But I can sing some nights too?"

"Yeah, as an opening act. You need a band to be a headliner."

A band. I don't know anybody who plays, other than Cap. Maybe I can put some feelers out. "Whatever I can get, I'd appreciate."

"Friday. Be here at four-thirty. You'll shadow another server. Play a twenty-minute set at seven. Then back to serving till we close."

"Okay. Thank you."

"Yep." He opens the door just a crack and closes it, a deep-set scowl across his brow. "If you're thinking of changing the status quo? Don't. It's better people think we don't know each other beyond you're Rowdy's sister, and I'm his friend. There's nothing more than that."

I suck in air, feeling light-headed, gripping the chair for support. "Landry—"

"Don't." The menace in his tone is surprising yet strangely not off-putting. "I've always known you recognized me. You prefer everyone thinks we're strangers. Let's keep it that way."

Damn, my gentle QB has grown into a tough-as-nails man who takes no shit. Even from me. I don't plan on him staying a stranger. I'd rather people not know about our past, but maybe, just maybe, I can get him to give me another chance so he can fall for me all over again. Only this time, I'll have to work for it.

"Okay. See you Friday."

The door opens just enough for me and my guitar case to slide out before quietly closing behind me. It takes a moment or two to get my bearings.

He's known all this time and never said anything to me or Rowdy. It truly did take me a minute at Rowdy's wedding to figure out "Cowboy," as everyone called him was my Landry. The same young man I fell in love with when he was only seventeen, me slightly younger. A fact he wouldn't be too happy to know since I told him we were the same age.

He's angry. He has a right to be. He'll be a whole lot angrier if he finds out the truth of what happened that fateful spring break and the months that followed. Why I left without a trace, never returned his calls, his texts.

I ghosted him.

And I've regretted it every day since.

CHAPTER 2

PAST ~ ONE MONTH AGO

SWIPE MY TREMBLING HANDS DOWN MY SHIRT, trying to smooth it out. I'm a sweaty mess, in need of a shower, food, a drink, and a good night's sleep on a comfortable bed or couch, anywhere but the floor or a cramped bus. Deciding my clothes are a lost cause, I pull my hair into a messy bun, a trick I learned from Cam. How many sisters learn how to do that from their brothers and not other girlfriends? Probably not many. But most guys don't have great hair like my brother.

I am a bit envious of the way he makes it look effortless. I, on the other hand, have to work hard to keep my thick locks from becoming a tangled disaster. I lose the battle most days. Especially today.

Ignoring my reflection in the shop window, I double-check the sign above the door, which reads *Sugarplums*, confirming I'm in the right place.

How sad is it that I don't have my brother's number memorized? I've felt helpless since I lost nearly all my belongings. But my phone was the most devastating loss. I didn't realize how reliant I was on technology until it was gone. And when I say "lost," I mean *stolen*.

I take a calming breath and open the door. Cool air and the smell of sweet deliciousness hit me simultaneously. My mouth salivates for a bite of anything chocolatey. I set my bags down and step closer, glancing at the display cases full of treats I'd like to dive into, roll around in, and gorge to my heart's content.

My stomach growls. When's the last time I ate? My parched throat reminds me it's been a while. Maybe yesterday? How can I not remember? Oh, it was that nice lady who gave me half her—

"Taylor?"

Startled, I swivel and sway on my feet, catching sight of Cher at the swinging door between the back and the front of her shop.

She's pregnant. Ready-to-burst pregnant. I'd forgotten. Cam mentioned it in passing, but he didn't know I… God, she looks good… and happy.

A familiar pang hits me square in the heart. "Hey!" I hide my fidgety hands in my back pockets, my reply entirely too enthusiastic.

"Hi." Her smile falters, concern flitting in her eyes as she takes in my disheveled state.

Maybe I shouldn't have come. Does she even remember who I am? It's been a while since we met at Cam's wedding, but she said my name. I blink, feeling light-headed. Maybe I should sit before I actually do fall into one of her glass cases.

Cher grips my arm. "You look like a stiff breeze could knock you over. You hungry? Need a drink?"

Food and drink? *Yes, please.* "I am a little hungry." *Do you have a side of beef I could devour and then chase it with that whole tray of double chocolate brownies I spotted in the display case?*

"Come on with me, honey. Let's get you settled in my office with some food."

Honey. My momma used to call me that. Sometimes.

I start to follow but stop, remembering my bags. I can't forget them. They're all I have.

"Jess?" Cher stops in the kitchen full of people eating and talking. Their fun ceases when all eyes land on us.

"Yes, Ma'am?" the big guy in the back replies.

"Could you make a sandwich and bring some waters to my office?"

"Sure thing." He eyes me. "Hey, Taylor, it's good to see you."

Does he know me? How do I know him? "Hey…"

"Jess," he reminds me. "We met at your brother's wedding."

I relax. "That's right. I'm sorry. I'm horrible with names. Plus," I motion around the kitchen, "I didn't expect to see any Black Ops guys here."

He laughs. "It's my day job." His attention moved back to Cher. "I'll bring the food right in. And, uh, that other thing will be here soon."

Other thing?

"Great. Thank you." Cher takes by bag, guiding me to the office in back where I collapse on the couch.

Oh my God, can I sleep here?

"You look tired. You want to lie down for a minute?"

Yes, but if I do, I'm not sure I'll wake up this century. "No. I'm good. I'm a little worn out from the road is all."

"Did you drive here?"

I didn't think this through. What should I say? I'm not ready… "Um, no. Not exactly."

"Does Rowdy know you're here?" She sits in her office chair, facing me.

"No." No one knows I'm here. I dropped out of sight two weeks ago. Did anyone notice? Not that I'd know, since I'm unintentionally technology-free.

I'm on the last half of the sandwich and my second bottled water when Cher pops to her feet. "I'll be right back."

I'm too focused on feeding my face to reply but still when I hear his voice.

"Everything alright, Plum?" The love and concern in his tone has me setting the food aside and taking in the big man who could be no one else other than Cam's father. The resemblance is unmistakable, and yet I missed it. Or maybe I sensed it at the wedding. I couldn't stop staring between the two of them. Their bond seemed stronger than boss and employee, their quiet exchanges riddled with emotion.

"Taylor?" Cap spots me. Elation mixed with concern flash across his face.

"Yep, Taylor is here." Cher tugs him into the office and shuts the door.

I swallow my last bite, needing to garner the strength to face the man. "Hi." I give a little wave and cringe. Pitiful.

He frowns, moving forward. "What's going on?" He scans me like he can see below my skin, determine if I'm as damaged as I look. "What happened?" He kneels in front of me. "Are you alright?"

The tenderness in his voice and searching eyes breaks the dam I'd managed to put around my emotions and fear from the last weeks. I shake my head, unable to verbalize what he wants to hear: *I'm okay.*

But I'm not.

I'm not okay.

My trembling sobs must convey it, as he doesn't hesitate. He wraps me in a powerful hug. "Whatever it is, we'll take care of it. Take care of *you.*"

When was the last time anyone said they'd take care of me?

I cry even harder when I realize the answer.

Keeping me close, he switches to sit on the couch and holds me and Cher as I can only cry uncontrollably and finally manage a squeaky, "I'm sorry."

"Shh, now. None of that. You're safe here. Always welcome." His gruff reply means more than he'll ever know.

"What happened, Taylor? Are you hurt?" Cher's emotion-laden concern penetrates my cries.

"I was robbed." I swipe at my face. "He took everything except those." I motion to my bag and guitar.

"Did he hurt you?" He moves so I'm facing him. Hands on my shoulders, his gaze flits up and down my body.

"No," my reply's a little too adamant. "H-he took my car, my purse, wallet, phone, everything I had except..." *What I have here.*

Cher squeezes my hand. "It's okay, honey. We'll get it sorted out. You can stay with us if you feel comfortable, or Rowdy—"

The door flies open, my brother filling the doorway. Jess gives me a sad smile over his shoulder. "What the fuck, Taylor?" Cam stomps forward, pulling me from Cap and sitting with me in his arms. "Are you okay?"

I sink into his hold, crying harder, unable to answer him. Thankfully, I don't have to. Cher fills him in.

"When was this?" Cam asks into my hair.

"Two weeks ago," I mumble.

"Two weeks!" Cap and Cam bark at the same time.

I jolt, curling into myself. I knew they wouldn't like that answer.

"Maybe we should let her get settled and talk details when she's had a chance to rest, eat a full meal…"

Sleep. I'd kill for a bed right now.

"She's right." Cam continues to rub my back. "Let's get you home. We can talk more later."

Sniffing, I pull back, cautiously eyeing the three of them. "Um… I'd like to stay with Cap and Cheryl, if that's okay?"

"What?" Cam is quick to reply.

"Of course it is," Cher and Cap echo.

I disentangle from Cam, giving myself room to take a shaky breath or two as I look between my brother and Cap. "I've known you all my life, Cam. I'd like to have a chance to get to know Cap and Cheryl. He is my dad too, after all." I drop the bomb I'm sure they were wondering if I knew.

"Fuck." My brother runs his hands over his face.

"Taylor, I'm sorry." Cap's gentle reply pings in my chest. This is my dad. My *real* dad.

"I'm not mad… Well, I am, but not at y'all. I just…" …*feel so alone and angry. Betrayed.*

Momma, why did you leave us with this mess?

I can't hold back my tears.

In a flash I'm in Cher's arms. As tiny as she is, her grip packs a punch.

"We don't have to talk about any of this until you're ready. Just know we're all here for you. Cap and I can't wait to get to know you better."

"Really?" I swipe at my tears. She speaks like I'm already *something* to her.

Cap is by my side, handing me a tissue. "I've been waiting to see you, get to know you since the second Rowdy told me you were mine too. You're welcome here in our home, in Rowdy's home, in any of our homes as long as you need—want to stay. You're family. We take care of our own."

We take care of our own resonates in my head on repeat as Cam drives me to Cap and Cher's home. They consider me one of theirs. I feared how they'd react. I never thought their response would be so open and accepting.

The ride is quiet, not uncomfortably so. Cam knows better than most I need time to get my head on straight before I'm ready to talk about Mom and the mess she left behind. Maybe he needs a minute to process too. After all, he didn't know I knew or that I was coming to visit.

I practically fall into the guestroom bed and consider sleeping for a month. Turns out I only get about twenty minutes before Cam wakes me up.

"Cher's in labor."

"What? Like now? We just saw her."

He laughs, handing me a cup of coffee. "That's kinda how it works, Tay. One minute you're feeling about as big as a house, and the next you're in labor. I don't think there's much build-up. At least, not in my experience."

I bury my guilt over not being here for the birth of his first child in a deep breath of coffee, blowing over the top till I dare take a sip. "Think I have time for a quick shower?"

He glances at the clock, me, the floor and back to me. "Be quick about it. I don't want to miss being there if they need me—us," he amends. "Jess will be here in a minute with the twins. He'll stay till we get back."

I nearly choke on my coffee. "Jess? As in MMA fighter and baker Jess?"

He nods, checking his phone. "Yep." His eyes fly to me. "I know you're..." He frowns, taking in my still disheveled state.

I didn't have the gusto to shower before lying down. I should have.

"...worn out," he concludes. "You don't have to go. They'll understand. But I can't miss being there. So, either get up or let me go."

"I'm coming. Hold your horses." When he doesn't budge from his spot next to the bed, I pointedly arch a brow. "Unless you want to see more of me than you'd care to, you need to leave. I think I was three the last time you saw me naked."

"Whoa, I'm leaving." He holds up his hand and turns away when I start to get up. "Actually, you were six. Decided you didn't want to wear your swimsuit in the pool that day. Said you wanted to go skinny dippin'."

Damn, the memory has tears prickling the back of my eyes. He had friends over too. I remember. I was braver then. Stupider too. "Those days are long over." I sigh over another sip of coffee. "Give me fifteen, and I'll be down."

He stops at the door, his head tilted to the side, eyes on the carpet. "Take twenty. And, Tay—" he pauses, the door nearly closed, "it's good to see you. No matter the circumstances or how you got here, I'm glad you are."

Yep, that has tears falling. "Love you," I eventually manage to whisper to the closed door, then take a deep breath and head to the shower. I can't get lost in my emotions. This is my chance to be a part of Cap's family, experience the birth of his daughter—my *sister*.

I can't blow this. This is the only family I have left.

CHAPTER 3

"CAN I GET YOU ANYTHING, CHER?" I HAND HER Baby Iris, fussing for her momma. I soothed her for as long as I could, but in the end, the one-month-old sweetie wants what only her momma can give—her breast.

In their bedroom, settled in bed, Cher cradles Iris in her arms and gets her latched with little effort. She's a pro at this, I suppose. Iris is her fifth kid, though there was a long break between Reese and the twins, Cade and Wade. Maybe it's like riding a bike; once you acquire the skill, you never forget.

"I'd love a cup of coffee and something to eat." Her smile is warm and always welcoming. I don't fully know her and Reese's story, but I know they've been working on their relationship. You'd never know it to see her with Reese and Gabriel or how she is one-hundred-percent present for her newest babies: Cade, Wade, and Iris, or how she is with Rowdy and Frankie—and even me—she treats us all like we belong to her, shared blood or not.

"You got it." I turn to go, only to be halted by Cap.

"*I've* got it, Taylor." He slips past me with a wink and sets the tray

of food on Cher's lap. "This is my job, Plum. Don't go giving it away."
He kisses her cheek and sits beside her on the bed.

Is he going to feed her? My eyes prick at the thought. Why can't I
find a guy like him?

Cher cups his hand before he stabs a bite of omelet. "I thought
Taylor could help you. That's all. I'm not giving anything away."

My heart pangs at the beauty in their love for each other. He's so
tender with her. I've never seen anything like it. Living here for the past
month, I've gotten to see this side of them. They don't hide their af-
fection with others around, but in the sanctuary of their home where
they're more open and relaxed, it feels intimate and private. I'm honored to be a part of it, in any way they let me, but I also don't want to
intrude.

"Taylor." Cap stops my emotional and actual retreat.

I turn to face them. "Yes?"

His back is still to me as he says, "Breakfast is on the stove. Please
eat something."

"Thanks. I will." I leave before either of them ask me what they've
been hinting at wanting to know since I arrived: *what happened?*

Iris' birth has given me a reprieve from having to share any details.
And I keep as busy as possible with my younger brothers and my new
sister, helping out at the bakery and at home as much as they'll let me,
and now my new job at Landry's bar—all in an effort to avoid my own
shit. The busier I am, the less time I have to think, and the less I think,
the better.

"If you give me thirty, I can drive you to the bakery."

My heart pounds in my ears, his voice is so close. I turn to find
him filling the doorway only a few feet away, his expectant gaze on me.
"I… uh, like to ride. If that's okay?"

His frown doesn't intimidate me like it did when I first met him.
He's a big man, like Cam, so his size doesn't scare me. I'm used to it.
His protectiveness doesn't overwhelm me either—also used to it from
my brothers—even Drake. It's his scowl—the idea of disappointing

17

him—*that* bothers me. I want to be someone he can be proud of. And I'm not that. Not yet.

He nods. "Don't forget your phone. There's money on the island. Take it. Don't forget to hydrate. Your thermos is next to the cash."

This man. He knew. I rush back and kiss his cheek, giving him a hug he's quick to return. "Thank you."

He kisses my temple. "You don't need to thank me. Just be careful. Call if you need me." He releases me, squeezing my hand as I step back. "Or if you want to talk."

Talk. Yeah, I don't want to do that. "I will." I start to leave but remember I never told them, "I start at Mel's bar tonight. So, I'll come home after the bakery to change, but I won't be here for dinner or around this evening."

Cap swipes something off the dresser behind him. "Take Cher's car." Her set of keys dangles from his finger.

I back away, hands up. I'm still not ready for that. "No. But thanks."

"How are you going to get there?" His frown is back.

I give him what I've been told is my award-winning smile. "I'll figure it out."

"Taylor," he grumbles as I descend the stairs.

"Don't worry, *Dad*. I got this," I toss over my shoulder.

His growl only makes me laugh. I pulled the dad card—and it felt good, despite the context. It was a cheap redirect, but it worked. I don't hear a peep from them before I leave.

"I'm giving you a ride home," Jess throws out before I even get a chance to say hello. His gaze flashes to the security monitor over my head where he must have seen me chaining my bike outside.

"I have a ride. But good morning to you too, sunshine."

"Hmph, morning. Still taking you home after your shift. Your *ride* will fit in the back of my truck." He points down the hall. "Don't forget to clock in."

Damn, I'd hoped no one noticed. I don't like taking money from Cher. She just had a baby, for goodness' sake. That wasn't cheap—the receipts I'd seen for diapers alone made me tense.

"After you clock in,"—he glares, making his point—"you can help Jam restock the cases. After that… you can help me."

"Sure thing." I put my bag in the office, keeping my thermos with me, clock in, wash my hands and don an apron. I sidle up next to Charlotte, who for some reason goes by Jam. I haven't gotten the story on that nickname. I have a feeling it's Jess' doing. He likes giving nicknames. I find it best not to ask questions, giving someone an opening to ask questions in return.

"Good morning."

"Hey, good morning. How is that little cutie today?" Jam beams, motioning to the *Call Me Chunky* bars that need to be restocked.

I grab the tray and start refilling. "She's beautiful. Oohing and cooing and getting cuter by the minute." Truly, I could get lost in her big blue eyes, just like her momma's. Don't get me started on her kissable cheeks. "She's got us all wrapped around her chubby little finger."

Jam laughs. "I know she does."

We work until the display cases are refilled from the early morning rush. Then I leave her to man the front as I slip into the kitchen to see what task Jess has for me. He's been teaching me the basics of making dough. I'm amazed at his knowledge and how many different types of dough and techniques there are based on what we're making. Most days I don't arrive early enough to make the first batches. It's usually on its second to third rise by the time I saunter in around eight in the morning.

"You amaze me, Jess." He's working another batch of his cinnamon roll dough as I work on coating the dough he prepared for me with butter, sugar, and cinnamon before it gets rolled, cut, and left to rise again before baking. "I don't even know how you keep it all straight: which rise a dough is on, which dough is what, what's in the oven. Warm hands and cold hands."

I know he has a system. He's explained it to me, shown me his timers with notes below each for what they're for, clips for the rise a dough is on, including the type of dough and how many rises it needs in total. He's like a well-oiled machine whose parts never stop working, never stop churning.

"Flattery will get you everywhere, Taytay." His muscles flex as he kneads the dough, flips it and slaps it on the counter with a loud *thwap*. Then he folds it into a ball, kneading, flipping, and slapping over and over again. Does he even need to work out after a day at the bakery?

"I'm not trying to go everywhere," I mumble mostly to myself.

"No? Where are you trying to go?"

I shrug while attempting to roll my buttered, sugared, cinnamoned dough into a long tootsie roll while ignoring his assessing gaze. "I don't know exactly. I think I'm trying to fit right where I am." I frown at my end product. It looks nothing like his examples.

"You'll get it. You're a natural." He sets the buttered extra-large cookie sheet in front of me.

"It's not tight enough," I muse, considering if I should unroll it and try again.

"That's what she said." He waggles his eyebrows, smirking.

So corny, I can't help but laugh. "You're a dork."

"Yep." He's proud of it too, making him even more endearing.

Motioning to my dough, he directs, "It's good. Cut it in half, and then in half again, until you get slices about an inch thick. Then place them on the cookie sheet and rack it to rise. Anything that gets messed up—doesn't look pretty but tastes amazing—we give as samples. No worries."

I bloom under his encouragement. It's a bonus he thinks it'll at least taste good. Nothing goes to waste here. It's either perfect to sell or just right for samples. I hope someday mine fall in the *perfect to sell* category.

When the baking is done and prep for tomorrow is complete, Jess gives me a ride home. It's not the first time he's given me a ride. I never told him where I was staying. He just knew. He's also never questioned why I'm living with Cap instead of Cam. I don't think it's common knowledge among the Black Ops guys that Cap is my father too. I haven't told anyone. I'm not hiding it, but it's not *only* my secret to tell since I'm the odd one coming into their lives. Plus, Cap has been a little busy with his newborn daughter being delivered the same day his first-born daughter arrived in town.

Her arrival trumps mine.

I'm not upset by that fact. It's how it should be. Also, the less prying into my life, the better.

"I'll pick you up at four," Jess advises as he pulls my bike out of the bed of his truck.

"And why would you do that?" I square my shoulders, needing to discern his motives.

He crosses his arms over his massive chest. "You sure as fuck aren't riding a *bicycle* home from a bar at three in the morning."

"I never told you I got a second job." Who told him?

There's no pity or deception in his eyes. "I heard you'll be working nights at Mel's. It's a nice enough, but nowhere in Vegas is safe riding home from in the middle of the night. It's not worth the cardio. You either need to drive yourself or let others help. Tonight, I'm your ride." With that, he walks away, leaving me stammering as he drives off.

"Thank you!" I holler before he reaches the end of the driveway.

He waves out the window. I guess he heard me.

Inside, the house is quiet. I grab a snack and head to my room to shower and get ready for tonight. It's my first night waiting tables. But it's not my first night singing in front of a crowd. I tried my hand at it a few times back home. Thank God.

Now, if only the man I wish would hear and see me would. That thought alone has the butterflies flapping in my tummy, and me considering for a moment that maybe working at Landry's bar is not the brightest idea. He hasn't been all that welcoming. I'm not even sure he can stand the sight of me.

Kill him with kindness, Mom's voice plays in my head.

Yeah, but maybe I should take the hint. I could realistically get a gig playing music at another bar, but this one feels safer than an unknown club, and that matters.

Maybe he and I are a lost cause better left in the past. Not all things are meant to be resurrected. Actually, most things aren't.

Ask for forgiveness.

"Shush. I don't remember asking you."

CHAPTER 4

OWNING MEL'S BAR HAS GIVEN ME A SENSE OF purpose I didn't know I was missing. I thought winning an MMA title was my goal. It turns out I need more. I need a place to call my own, where I call the shots. Where I don't get beat up or bested on my worst day or mess someone else up on my best day. Where I can hang and talk shit, or disappear into my office or my apartment above and know I'm only seconds away from companionship if I want it—need it.

Mel must have known, sensed it. The more I feel like it's my bar and not Mel's hand-me-down, the more at peace I feel. Completing the renovations a few months ago was the beginning of making Mel's mine, putting my stamp on the new booths and tables. The stage is still too small, but I can't do anything about it without knocking down walls and expanding into the back parking lot. Maybe in a few years. The chefs love the new ovens and cooktop. The griddle stayed as it was well seasoned in a good way and only adds to the flavors of the food coming off it.

Mel's would be perfect if it weren't for the controversial blonde messing with my mojo. With her inescapable invasion of my sanctuary, I'm restless and downright cranky.

I was fine—fucking fantastic—until she darkened my bar with her golden glow and Texas swagger, the extent of which I'd nearly forgotten. I'd nearly buried her memory, almost erased her imprint on my life from my thoughts, purged her from my soul.

I was so close.

Close only counts in horseshoes and hand grenades.

Maybe it's more accurate to say she dropped a grenade on my life the day she ghosted me at seventeen. I've been trying to put the pieces back together ever since. Maybe that's what I was *close* to doing.

She rattled the cage, cracked the repairs at Rowdy's wedding, but she damn near demolished them the moment she showed up to audition in my bar. *My* bar. Of all the gin joints…

One note was all it took for me to know I'd never have peace in Mel's again. She tainted my world with her sinful voice, poisoned my soul with each painful word she may or may not have intended for me.

I nearly polish a hole in the bar before Ruby slides in, hip-checking me. "Do I really have to train the new girl? Why can't Trish do it?"

That's right, it's Friday. *She* starts today. I pretend I haven't been counting down the days, the minutes, the eternities till I'd see her again.

"Because I told you to do it." I turn, putting distance between us, which only ends up placing me face-to-face with said *new girl* I'm not supposed to know.

Fucking fantastic.

I wipe down this side of the bar as if it needs it, giving my eyes something to focus on besides her. Riotously, my eyeballs don't obey and insist on scanning her in her Mel's Bar T-shirt that's knotted at the waist, making it skintight and revealing her flat belly and silky skin I still remember the taste of; long, toned legs that used to wrap around me on display in her cutoffs; and damn sexy black cowboy boots.

Fuck. Me.

Taylor opens her mouth to say something I don't want to hear. I cut her off before I suffer through her kind greeting or inane question. "See Leo."

Hurt flashes in her eyes. My stomach twists. I can't deal, so I about-face and nearly smash Ruby against the beer dispenser. "You don't belong back here. You're not a bartender or a manager." I point to the gap in the bar. "Out."

"Dang, so grumpy. I'm going. I'm going." Ruby holds her hands up and slips away, frowning between Taylor and me before pasting on the bright smile that gets her loads of tips and regulars hoping to be on the receiving end of more than just her smile. She uses it to her advantage.

With a half-hearted wave, she greets Taylor, "Hey, I'm Ruby. Leo is in the back. I'll show you."

"Hi. I'd appreciate that. I'm Taylor, by the way," the heartbreaker cheerfully replies.

I pour a shot of the first liquor my hand lands on and down it before the click of her cowboy boots fades away. I cringe at the taste—peach schnapps. Not my go-to drink—but I relish the sweet goodness all the same.

"You alright, man?" Jake eyes the shot glass I'm still gripping, considering taking another.

I rarely drink while working. Actually, I *never* drink while working. "Peachy."

He chuckles. "Yeah, that's obvious." His gaze flashes to where the girls disappeared and back to me. "Something I ought to know?"

I shoot half a shot and slam it on the bar top. God, people really drink that shit? "Not a damn thing."

I busy myself being sure the tables are ready to go, bathrooms are stocked, and the kitchen is prepped and ready—basically all the stuff I pay other people to do. I need to talk to Leo, but not while he's talking to Ruby and Taylor, hence my little dance around my bar. If Ruby knew I had feelings for Taylor, she would eat Taylor for a midnight snack, not that I have anything going on with Ruby. She's a little headstrong and has a hard time accepting I don't want to fuck her.

I don't need my employees knowing my business. Plus, I'm not the only one impacted.

When Walker, my MMA teammate and bouncer, arrives with a fist bump a few minutes before the doors are unlocked, I start to relax. He and his guys will keep everyone in line. Not that I can't, but I can't be all places all the time, and tonight, I'm working the bar with Jake. I want to keep an eye out for Taylor. I may not want her here, but I sure as shit don't want anything or anyone making her feel unwelcomed—besides me, that is—or worse, feeling they have a right to get cozy just because she's the new shiny toy in town.

She's nobody's fucking toy.

Especially not mine.

And that pisses me off even more.

I don't want her anymore—she's been out of my system for years!

Yep, that's the lie I'm sticking to.

It's not long before my band arrives and sets up on the stage, leaving room for the opening act—which happens to be Taylor. I twitch, wanting to take another shot or step out back for a smoke—and I don't even smoke, so that uncharacteristic urge says a lot. We're swamped, and I can't do more than give the band quick nods of acknowledgment. After my band settles in the back booth, always reserved for the headlining entertainment, Taylor and Ruby get them a round of drinks.

Leo steps up to the bar a little before seven, calling me to the side. We're nearly to compacity; there is no *to the side* available. I bend closer to make out what he's saying, "I don't know if she's gonna make it on stage without throwing up. She's shaking like a leaf."

I follow his gaze to Taylor, barely visible to the side stage—as small as it is, staring out at the mass of people all waiting for the opening act.

Live music is a big draw here. We don't charge extra—two-drink minimum for a table. We don't have a cover to get in. We offer live music three nights a week, and, by request, most of those nights are my band. Mel gave us a chance, barely formed after I moved here from California when Cap recruited me for his Black Ops MMA team. Not a single day goes by that I'm not thankful for that chance. But singing on stage—some original songs, most are covers—is another puzzle piece clicking into place in the menagerie of my life. I'm not one thing. I'm many things. All pieces seem to be required to find joy and satisfaction—though, admittedly, there's still a huge piece missing, and she's standing right there on that stage like all she wants to do is run from the opportunity to shine.

I pat him on the shoulder. "Help Jake till I get back." I slip around him as he gets behind the bar.

Taking the stairs two at a time, I pull my jittery songbird to the side, cornering her between the wall and the side curtain, ignoring her as she gasps, "Landry, what are—"

"Listen." I bend low, my lips grazing her ear. Her little hands, gripping my shirt at my waist, remind me and my body what it felt like when she was mine. "You can go home. Pretend tonight never happened. Get a job as a lawyer or whatever you did back in Texas. You don't have to do this."

"I do." She presses her forehead to my chest, shaking like a scared little bird I've never seen before. It only angers me. Not at her, but at whatever life did to her since I knew the bolder version of her when we were seventeen.

I want to hold her until she stills and softens in my arms, but I can't. It's not what either of us need. I can't be that guy for her. There was a time I would have roped the moon for her, but now...

I tip her chin till her eyes are on me. "Then you have to suck it up. Remember why you want this job. Why you brought your guitar all the way from Texas. You hold it like it's precious—it means something to you. Go out on that stage and make her sing. *Show* them why you're here."

She opens her mouth and shakes her head to protest, to give excuses or explain why she feels she can't. Instead of letting her, I give her something else to think about, other than her fear.

CHAPTER 5

H IS LIPS CRASH OVER MINE, STEALING MY BREATH—
my sanity. It's not a quick peck. It's not a lazy Sunday morning or
a frenzied Friday night. It's somewhere between heaven and hell,
between hope and despair, between desire and pity. Like I've been doing
since I walked away from him all those years ago, this kiss existing in the
in-between, between living and dying.

And dying.

And dying.

On a ragged breath, he pulls away, his forehead pressed to mine. "Go
show them whatcha got, songbird." One more press of his mouth to mine,
then he steps back, hands me my guitar, and leaves on a whispered, "Fuck."

I want to giggle and touch my lips.

He kissed me.

He may hate me, but a part of him definitely does not. A bud of hope
springs free. Maybe there's a chance for us after all. If he didn't care, he
wouldn't have come to give me a pep talk, and he certainly wouldn't have
kissed me. I'll have to show him I'm worth forgiving. But first, I have to
convince myself. Step one: Get out there and sing.

Leo winks as he passes, heading for the microphone.

Did he see Landry kiss me? Does it show on my face?

Leo's introduction is short and sweet. Before I know it, I'm stepping out of the darkness and into the light of the stage. I slip the guitar strap over my head, strum a few chords to be sure my girl is still in tune. Just the motion, the sound it produces, calms the nerves.

The crowd graciously whoops, claps, and whistles as I near the mic. I take a deep breath, letting it out slowly, wishing the stage lights were brighter so I couldn't see their eyes all on me, curious and hungry. The room sizzles with electricity. Cam said the live band nights are crazy, but I didn't expect it to be like this. Not for my first time…

"Come on, sweetheart," some guy yells from a table in back. I realize it's one of the band guys I served earlier, not heckling but encouraging.

I smile and nod, strum a few chords, then work my way into the opening of We Three's "Lifeline."

As I hit the bridge, the crowd fades away. The only face I see is Landry's. He's trying to not watch, not listen, but he can't resist. Our draw is inescapable. It always has been. I fear it always will be.

What will I do if he never forgives me?

Will I ache for him forever?

I moved here to be with my new family and maybe my old flame. Surely that means something.

My voice cracks with emotions when I sing about giving up. His eyes flash to me after having looked away to serve a guy at the bar, but I can't keep his gaze. I break contact as I continue, saying a silent prayer to just make it through this song and the ones that follow.

I avoid looking in his general vicinity for the rest of my set. It's too much—*he's* too much. My emotions, my memories surrounding us are raw and jagged, and dangerous territory, loaded with ticking timebombs.

Before I know it, I manage to make it through my playlist without giving in to the barren hole in my heart or letting the memories steal my voice, my moment to shine on stage. I wrap up my set to cheers and hoots. I smile and curtsy like an idiot, thanking them and hurrying off the stage, making a beeline for the employee lounge to put my guitar away and take a moment to tame my riotous, bittersweet emotions.

Behind me, as I close the door, Leo is at the mic telling the crowd to *give it up* for me one more time before he announces the house band, who I hear is really good and the main draw on live music nights.

With my emotions stuffed back inside where they belong and not openly traipsing inside my glassy eyes or along my face, I head out to find Ruby to shadow for the rest of the night. But I only make it a step or two before I'm engulfed in strong arms and lifted off the ground.

Panic doesn't have time to rise before the behemoth holding me whispers in my ear, "You sing like a fucking angel, Taytay."

I release a shaking breath and relax against Jess' chest as he sets me on my feet. I don't get a chance to reply before my gaze locks on the hazel eyes shining my way from on stage. Landry is front and center, his lips brushing the mic as he plays guitar and sings with blazing daggers flicking between Jess and me.

Ohmylawd. "I didn't know he sang and played too," I whisper to no one in particular.

Coming to stand beside me, Jess slings his arm over my shoulder. "Yeah, our boy is full of wicked talent. You should see him throw a football."

Yep, that one I knew. He was his high school's star quarterback. He didn't talk about it much, but I looked him up when I got home from Padre Island, where we met on spring break. He had a promising football career ahead of him. What made him change his mind and go for mixed martial arts instead? And own this place. I glance around the packed bar. He was destined to do more with his life.

Did I do anything to help inspire his change in direction?

"I gotta get back to work." I kiss Jess on the cheek and catch sight of Ruby at the bar placing an order. "See you later."

"Laters. Oh." Jess grips my wrist. "Walker is gonna give you a ride home."

I frown. "I don't need a ride."

He steps into me, his brow furrowed. "You don't have your bike, and

I wouldn't let you ride it home, anyway. I'll call Cap and Rowdy if you don't let Walker."

That's a low blow. But I don't need those two here tonight. The situation is messy enough as it is. I can handle them on my own, but Landry and I haven't been in such close proximity of each other with Rowdy and Cap since their weddings. "Okay. Thanks." I hurry off before he can demand anything else of me.

Sidling next to Ruby, I cut off whatever she's about to say by asking, "How can I help?"

"You can take these beers to the table behind us, then check on their food." She provides the table number in case I forgot their numbering system. I didn't forget. I just don't have it memorized yet.

"On it." I grab the beers and a couple of extra cocktail napkins and work my way to the designated table, dropping off their drinks and letting them know I'm going to check on their food.

When I come out of the kitchen with their meals, the band slides into a slower tune, an acoustic version of "What Hurts The Most." I saw Aaron Lewis perform it live years ago. I thought his version was so much better than the original by Rascal Flatts. Hearing Landry sing it now puts both versions to shame. His voice is sultry and raspy with a rich vibrato. I want to stop and listen, give him my full attention. I shouldn't. He doesn't want that, right? Plus, I have food to deliver and many more tables to check on.

He kissed you.

I stumble at the memory. That all-too-familiar ache rising to the surface. He only kissed me to distract me from my stage fright. The man wants nothing to do with me. I'm certain I only got this gig because of my family connections. If he had his way, I never would have been allowed to step food in the door.

Worse, maybe he was only trying to score points with them by hiring me...

I drop off the food and turn, trying to find Ruby in the sea of people. When I don't find her, I dare to steal a glimpse of Landry and his band.

Just one look. Then back to work.

Only, his eyes are already on me like he was waiting, and, as if on cue, his rich voice packs a wallop with the next line of the song, saying it's hard dealing with the pain of losing me…

Is he doing this on purpose? Did he choose that song for me? It struck me like he did, whether he meant to or not. I swallow the lump in my throat and blink away the tears. Hiding my face, I dart away to find Ruby. There's work to do, and crying over my past—over him—isn't going to get it done.

I knew seeing him would be hard. I just didn't anticipate it hurting this much. Coming face-to-face with his hurt and anger, digging up my failures and disappointments. It's all so inescapable.

But I knew that, right? I came to Vegas to get to know Cap, my little brothers and sister, and my nephew, but I also stayed for Landry—and a teensy bit for me.

Nothing worthwhile is gained without sacrifice. Thank you, Doctor Martin Luther King Jr.

I pray this sacrifice doesn't bite me in the ass.

CHAPTER 6

MOMMA SAYS STARING IS RUDE. BUT LAWD HELP me, this boy is fine and built like a dually truck on steroids. His friends aren't bad-looking either, but Dually has the surfer-guy look down pat: tan from head to toe, boardshorts hanging low on his narrow waist and a glimpse of his deep V, and dirty-blond hair that's longer and lighter on top. The way he flips his head to get it out of his eyes is doing strange things to my insides, particularly my nether regions, which I've dreamt about using, but I don't have much practical experience. I'm rocking it theoretically, though.

Mandy elbows me. "You got a little something right here." She points to the corner of her lips.

I swipe at my mouth. There's nothing there.

"You're drooling, Taylor. You gotta be more sophisticated than that, or they'll never think we're older than we are. Don't make it too easy."

Easy. She's one to talk. She already hooked up with a guy not thirty minutes after we checked into our hotel. I swear Mandy is either going to be president one day or a teen mom before she turns sixteen. It's a tossup. Maybe even both.

"I'm sophisticated." I throw my wavy blonde hair over my shoulder and glance the other way. "They don't even know we exist. It doesn't hurt to look when no one is watching."

"Think again."

Dually catches the football not five feet from my head. I sputter when a little sand flies in my mouth.

His head jerks my direction. "Oh, shit. Sorry."

I wave him off, but he's already running the other way, tossing the ball back to his buddy.

I'm not paying attention when a shadow falls over me seconds before Dually plops down next my beach towel. He pushes his sunglasses up to rest on his forehead as he hands me a bottled water. "Sorry about the sand."

I don't tell him we have a cooler full of drinks. *His* water will taste better anyway, I'm sure. "Thanks." I twist the top off and take a long quenching drink, feeling his eyes on me the entire time.

When I lick my lips, catching an errant drop, he offers his hand. "I'm Landry Pierce."

I shake his hand, warm and firm. "Taylor."

He smirks when I don't give him my last name. I don't know him. He's cute and all, but so was Ted Bundy. My momma taught me to not stare—which I kinda already broke that rule, but she also told me not to give my full name to strangers. Okay, she told me not to talk to strangers, but given I know his name now, how much of a stranger can he be?

"It's nice to meet you, Taylor No-Last-Name." He motions over his shoulder to our beachfront hotel. "Are y'all staying here too?"

Too? I bite my lip. Should I tell him where we're staying?

"Yep. The four of us," Mandy pipes up, introducing herself and pointing to our other friends tossing a frisbee.

Landry does the same, his friends waving as he calls out their names. "We're going to the Crab Shack later. Y'all want to join us?" He eyes me then Mandy.

There are four of them and four of us. The place he's talking about is only a few minutes down the beach. We haven't made dinner plans, having only arrived a few hours ago. We do have to eat. "Sure. Sounds good."

His smile grows as he fishes his phone out of his pocket. "Here, text yourself so I have your number. I think we'll head in to shower and change in like an hour. But I'll touch base with you in case I don't see you before I leave."

"Ah, better places to go just now?" I tease.

His smirk is back. "No, actually. I just didn't want to come on too strong. I'm perfectly content to sit here with a beautiful woman at my side."

Good answer.

I text myself from his phone and hand it back. He sends me a text in return, and we both create a new contact.

For the next hour or so, we enjoy the beach, talk, chat with our friends, share secret glances and find ways to accidentally—or not so accidently—touch each other. By the time we head inside to get cleaned up, we're definitely no longer strangers, and I'm in dire need of a cold shower. Landry has flirting down to a science, and I'm happy to be the focus of his attention.

"Come on, Songbird, we're going to be late," Landry calls as I finish up in the bathroom. We got back to the hotel late, splitting up to shower and dress. As guys do, he beat me in getting ready. Mandy let him in before she left with the girls.

"I'm coming." I step out of the bathroom, twisting the skirt of my blue sundress, wondering if it's too much for a beach bonfire. What if he wants to go swimming? I could wear shorts and a tank top with my swimsuit underneath.

He stands, jaw ticking, his hands fisted at his side. "Damn, baby. You're a knockout."

The heat of my blush creeps up my chest to my face, making me feel sunburned. "It's not too much?"

"No. But now I don't want to go anywhere. I want to keep you to myself, see if you'll let me get you outta that dress."

Holymotherfullofgracewhat? Goosebumps run up my legs. "Landry." *Oh, and yes, please.*

He's been nothing but a gentleman these past few days. We only met four days ago, but since that first hello, we've spent every second of it together, friends be damned. Sleep, who needs it? It feels like I've known him my whole life. And I want to spend the rest of it getting to know everything about him.

He's in front of me before I catch my next breath. "Not kidding, Songbird. I don't much feel like sharing you tonight."

I reach behind me, turning the deadbolt, and flip the security guard just in case someone comes back early. "Can we order room service later?"

He captures my cheek. "Taylor, I'll order you every dang thing on the menu if you just say *yes*."

That's too easy. "Yes."

His breath is ragged by the time he closes the distance between his mouth and mine. "Whatever happens is up to you." He presses his lips to mine but doesn't deepen the kiss. "Got it?"

I nod, but if he thinks I'm putting on the brakes, he's crazy. "Got it." I practically tackle him, wrapping my arms and legs around him. Thankfully he's big and strong and can handle anything I throw at him. Not literally—well, except myself—I'm totally throwing myself at him. "Now get naked, Dually. I want to see a cock up close and personal-like."

"Jesus, Taylor. You can't say things like that. I'm desperate for you." He squeezes my ass, drawing my girly parts along his hardened ones. I shudder, tightening my legs around him. "You're gonna kill me, aren't you?" he whispers across my lips.

"Not before we finally have sex, I'm not." I kiss his neck, untangling myself from his body and start unbuttoning his shorts, tugging at his shirt at the same time.

"I was being a gentleman. Didn't want you to think I only liked you for your body."

"Like me for my body. Love me for my heart."

He stills my hands. "Taylor, I do. I do love you." His hazel eyes shimmer above mine, greener than usual, with sincerity ringing through every delectable inch of him.

He's gone all genteel on me. "Love you too, Landry. Honest, I do, but more naked and less talking."

"Jesus, fuck," he gasps when I grip his shaft before I even get his underwear off.

Knowing how I affect him only makes me hotter for him and his hardness in my hand. "Touch me like you did the other night, only this time use your mouth too." I've never come so hard as I did when he got me off with his fingers. I thought I was going to die.

"Taylor," he growls.

"Yes." I kiss his cheek, nibbling from his jaw to his mouth. "I love it when you get all growly. It does things to me."

He stops me from pumping him like a ketchup bottle. "On the bed. Now."

I unzip my dress, letting it drop to the floor as I walk to the bed in only my mint green thong, casting a wanton gaze over my shoulder and a smile tipping my lips. I'm giddy and nervous like a girl getting ready to have sex for the first time with the boy she loves. How perfect is that?

When he comes down over me, I forget how to breathe until he caresses my cheek, understanding warming his gaze. "I've got you, Songbird. Tonight, we're gonna learn a whole new song together."

CHAPTER 7

THE POUNDING IN MY HEAD MAKES ME THINK THE place is under construction again until I realize the banging is my body's protest against too many shots that eased into beers after we closed out our set last night.

I know better than to drink while training. Hell, I'm *always* in training. I have been my whole life. First it was football. Now it's MMA. Always that nagging fear if I don't have a physically demanding life, I'll fall into drinking every night like my old man and his old man.

It's ironic, then, that I own a bar, and both my father and grandfather were killed by a drunk driver on their way to an AA meeting, working their sobriety each day, a breath at a time. Not that I knew firsthand. He left me and my mom for greener pastures when I was just a kid. We heard the news from my grandma—on my eighteenth birthday. Happy birthday to me.

Groaning like I'm a hundred and seven years old, I stagger to the kitchen and down two glasses of water before jumping in the shower. I feel nearly human by the time I get out and throw together my protein shake and food for the day.

It's after eleven when I step into the Black Ops gym, finding Rowdy and Gabriel lifting and Jonah working with a new guy on the bag.

When Rowdy's eyes lock on me, all I can think is, *I fucked your sister.*

Guilt eats at my gut as I drop my stuff in the locker room, only bringing my water and towel with me on the gym floor.

Gabriel has some grunge shit playing through the speakers. It does have a mean beat, which is why he picks it. Always know who gets here first by the music playing. With my late hours at the bar, I'm never the first here. I'm surprised to see Rowdy and Gabriel at all. They're early morning crew, usually gone before I arrive.

"Sleep in?" my hello to the two of them.

Gabriel's brows meet in the middle of his forehead. "Someone had a rough night. I thought it was me. I'm doing pretty good compared to you."

Wait till I start sweating, you'll get a good whiff of alcohol leaving my body through my pores. "I could use more sleep."

"Then why are you here?" Rowdy lies back on the bench press with Gabriel spotting him.

"To see your smiling faces." I grab the jump rope and start off slow, feeling the weight of last night's choices. No more drinking. From now on, it's Gabriel's one-drink-a-week rule, and only on Friday nights, unless it's fight week, then no drinking at all.

I don't even know when my next match is. I pulled out of the last two, feigning work stuff, which wasn't entirely a lie. I could have made it work, but having Taylor show up here—in my world—has derailed my concentration and dulled my vision. Color only seems to be in my life when she's near; without her—now that I remember what it's like to be in her presence—everything is shades of gray and muted tones. I've lost my zest, and I have idea how to get it back.

Starting to pick up speed with the rope, I sweat it out as Rowdy steps next to me, wiping his face with a towel. "Thanks for giving Taylor a chance. I heard things went well last night."

I grunt my response, keeping my eyes forward, concentrating on not tripping on my thoughts of his sister or the fact that I kissed her last night to ease her nerves. Or because I just couldn't stand the fear in her eyes. Fuck. Me. I'm still hung up on her like aging beef.

I come to a halt. He deserves more than my half-assed response. "She did great. You should come see her perform." I'm surprised he wasn't there to support her in the first place.

"Yeah, she made me promise not to come. But maybe I'll sneak in when she's on again." He starts in on the free weights.

"Wednesday." I take a drink of water and get back to the rope.

"What?" His weight freezes mid-curl, his focus all on me.

Don't look guilty. "The crowd loved her. She'll open on Wednesdays and Fridays going forward."

His smile is big and proud. It makes my heart hurt knowing how much he loves his sister, but it's his dimples that straighten my spine. They're identical to Taylor's... and Cap's. Did their mom have dimples too?

"I know you're working tonight, and tomorrow's your only day off, but we're having a cookout. Think you can come?" The invite comes from Rowdy, but Gabriel is watching like he's invested in my answer.

Sunday is the only day the bar is closed. I've thought about keeping it open all seven. But I need a break, and given I live above the place, it would be hard to take a day off knowing work is happening below my feet.

Before Taylor's arrival, I would have jumped at the chance to hang with these guys. I've admired them since joining the Black Ops team nearly three years ago, and Gabriel, I knew of him long before Cap came looking for me. I was lucky enough to be Gabriel's sparring partner before his title win. I'm honored and lucky to be here. "Yeah, man. What can I bring?"

"Nothing. Just you." Rowdy gets back to lifting.

Gabriel gives a smile and a slow nod of approval. What would I have gotten if I'd said *no?*

After my workout and shower, I find Cap in his office. Since he's become a family man, he's not here often on the weekends, but he greeted us before heading to his office to take care of a few things. I knock on his open door before entering.

His head pops up, and a quick smile cracks his normally stern face when he spots me. "Come in. Sit."

I didn't know Cap for long before he was together with Gabriel's mom Cher. But I've been around him enough to note his gentled disposition. He's still a tough MF when he needs to be, but to see him with his wife and kids, it gives me hope that it's never too late to find my own family beyond the makeshift one he's made me a part of.

"What's on your mind, son?" Setting his work aside, he leans back, giving me his full attention.

I sit in a chair opposite his desk, back straight, keeping eye contact. "I'm sorry about my fight status. I wasn't in a good headspace and didn't want to disappoint you—let the team down. But I'm ready, when you are, to get back in the game."

"You sure?" He spins a pen on the tips of his fingers. "There's no shame in taking time when you need it. Better to be safe than sorry."

I thought he might give me a hard time, tough love sort of thing. I should have known he'd understand. He's rarely unreasonable. I don't know his whole story, but he's a good man. Generous with his time, his commitment in helping everyone around him become the best version of themselves. "I'm sure. But if you need me to take a few practice bouts, I'm good with that. I'll prove myself."

He drops his pen and leans forward, piercing me with his green gaze. "Landry, you don't have to prove yourself to me. You did that before I asked you to join my team. You earn your spot every day whether you're actively taking fights or not."

"Yes, sir. I appreciate that."

"Good. Let me take a look and see what I can work out. Give me a few days."

"Yep, no problem." I stand and offer my hand. "Thanks, Cap. It's an honor to be here."

He stands and takes my hand, squeezing, not letting go. "You don't have to keep thanking me, Landry. I'm glad you're happy to be here, 'cause

I'm damn glad you are. You're family." He releases my hand with a quick shake.

His words hit home, bouncing around in my fatherless soul, chipping away at the empty, filling it up. I always ate up my coaches' approval, lived, preened under it, and died a thousand deaths when I let them down. Cap is no different. Yet *his* approval means more. I'm not sure why, maybe because this is my second chance, or I'm older now and know what it's like to lose it all.

"Are you coming to the cookout tomorrow?" he asks before I can slip out his door.

"Yep, I'll be there."

"Good, bring your guitar. Maybe we can play together if you're up to it."

"Sounds good." He's never heard me play. I haven't heard him, just noise from Rowdy and Gabriel about him surprising everyone by pulling out his guitar shortly after his twin boys were born. I guess it was an old passion he'd forgotten he loved until he opened his heart to loving Cher.

I wonder if he's played with Taylor? Is it awkward for her hanging out together knowing Cap is Rowdy's real father instead of sharing the same father with her? They thought they were full siblings. Turns out they're only half related.

I guess I'll find out tomorrow, assuming she'll be there.

Fuck. Taylor's going to be there.

Maybe I should back out. No-show it.

No, I've spent too much time letting her derail my life. No more.

I said I was ready to fight. Now I have to prove it, and that starts outside the ring.

CHAPTER 8

I SPEND THE MORNING HELPING CHER PREP FOOD TO take to Cam and Reese's, keeping my toddler brothers occupied, and snuggling Baby Iris when she's not attached to Cher's breasts or asleep. I've just gotten Cade and Wade in their highchairs with a mid-morning snack when Cap arrives with sweets from the bakery.

"I got the last Death by Chocolate cake." He leans in and kisses Cher on the neck. "Hey, Plum."

"Cap." She giggles when he hugs her from behind, pushing her into the counter. "Behave."

"Do I have to?" he grumbles, pats her butt and ambles over to the twins. "Hey, Slugger." He kisses Cade on the head, catching his hand before he pops him in the face. "Good try."

Then he kisses Wade, who giggles and wraps his fingers in Cap's hair, not letting go. "Hey, little lover, how you doin'?" He kisses Wade on the cheek, and that seems to be what Wade wanted, as he lets go of Cap's hair, offering him a Cheerio instead. Cap pretends to eat his hand, making the twins burst in a fit of giggles.

It's a sight I can't take my eyes off. Cap is such a big guy and yet so loving and gentle with his family. His gaze slides to me as he stands. "Hey, Tay." He wraps me in his arms, holding tight.

I stutter a breath and hug him back. "Hey," I barely manage around my rising emotions. I've been hugged more in the last month than I have my entire life.

"Don't think I forgot about you." He kisses my head. "Never." He gives me a knowing smile when he steps back, glancing around the room. "Where's Itty Bitty?"

"Napping," Cher and I respond in unison.

Cher checks the clock. "She'll be up soon."

"I'll get her when she does." He claps, rubbing his hands together. "What can I do to help?"

Cher puts him to work loading the diaper bags with food, bottles, sippy cups, and all the accoutrements needed for three babies under the age of eighteen months. It not only takes a village to raise kids. Apparently, it takes one to carry all their necessities too.

Once everything is ready, we load up. I squeeze into the third row of Cher's Escalade since the second row is overrun with baby seats.

Cap sticks his head in, frowning. "You okay back there? You can drive my truck if you want."

"Nope. I'm good." I sit on my hands to stop their endless fidgeting at the mere thought of getting behind the wheel. Somedays it hard to even be a passenger.

He nods, his frown not letting up. "I hope you know you can talk to me, Cher, or we can find you someone to talk to if you want. But you're going to have to drive eventually—"

Am I though? I glance out the window, catching Cher's caring gaze. Nothing gets past these two. They've experienced too much pain not to notice it in others. No wonder my mom loved this man. I blink away my tears.

"You can't ride a bike everywhere, especially not with the late hours you're working. We can get you a car. Start out slow, build up to driving to the bakery or Mel's."

My heart is trying to leap out of my chest. This is the most he's said about me not driving since I arrived. I appreciate his concern. It's not easy to admit, "I'm not ready. Maybe in a few weeks." Plus, I can't afford to buy a car right now.

"Has Barrett cut you off? Is that why you're working two jobs? We're happy to help in every way you'll let us."

"You have to stop being so nice to me." I sweep a tear away, only another falls. How different would my life be if I'd grown up with this man instead of Barrett?

He reaches back and squeezes my hand. "Never gonna happen, Taylor. I'm so happy you're here, that you're giving me and Cher this time to get to know you, and you us. You're all grown, but give me a little time to treat you like a teenager who needs her old man to buy her a car and take care of her."

Who can say no to that? "Okay, but there's no rush."

"It's settled. I'll start looking this week."

"Really there's no hurry. I don't even know if I can—"

He squeezes my hand. "It'll be here for when you are."

I manage to compose myself by the time we arrive a few streets over at Cam's massive house. It's not as big as our home in Texas, but it's the biggest in the neighborhood by far.

Cam, Jess, and Walker rush out to greet us and help carry everything inside. With Jess' arm slung over my shoulder, we enter the kitchen.

Over Reese's head I find one Landry "Cowboy" Pierce, and he looks pissed as hell. His hazel gaze flicks between Jess' arm and me, then he storms out back.

"Excuse me," I say to no one in particular and hurry after him.

"You've got it all wrong." My Heartbreaker steps before me as I gaze out over the lake, purposely keeping far away from the party going on behind me.

I don't look at her. I don't take in her green eyes that pierce my heart, or the cutoffs that show off her spectacular legs, or her soft pink lips I kissed only two days ago. "Do I?"

She crosses her arms. "Yeah, you do. Jess and I are just friends. He gives me rides. He's supportive."

My eyes narrow in on hers. "I bet he gives you rides." Nothing against Jess. He's a great guy. He's just not the guy for her.

Her hands fall at her sides. "To work. He gives me rides to *work*, and Walker drives me home from Mel's."

WTF? "I didn't realize you need to be chauffeured around, Ms. O'Dair."

She arches a brow, popping her hip. "It's Ms. *Permian*-O'Dair."

"Whatever." I'm done. I never should have come, knowing she was going to be here. We need to keep our contact to a minimum, and hanging out outside of work is not aligned with that. I turn to walk away, put as much space between us as possible.

She grabs my hand, sending sparks zipping up my arm.

"Please," she pleads, tugging me to a halt. She eases closer, my eyes locked on our contact. She's not letting go. I can't seem to do it either. "I hate this. Please, don't be mad at me. Don't hate me. Because I could never hate you."

"I don't hate you." I release her hand and fold my arms over my chest to keep from wrapping her in them. "To hate would mean I care."

I'm such an asshole.

She swallows hard, blinking up at me. So innocent and yet such a vixen.

A heartbreaker.

"You care." She seems certain.

"Don't be so sure. Eight years is a long time, sweetheart. I forgot all about you the minute you ghosted me."

Her chin trembles, and I have to look away.

There's no future for us. I have to be sure we both remember that.

"No you didn't," she whispers. "What we had—"

"Was just a fuck. Get over yourself." This time I don't stop when she calls my name. I head straight for the beer cooler and break my new rule of only one drink a week. I'll start tomorrow. I need something to smother the ache in my chest. I'm not sure if it's the existing hole she put there, or if it's new from making her cry.

Fuck. I really didn't intend on being so mean. That wasn't my intention when I arrived.

"Go easy." Gabriel comes to stand beside me seconds before Jess brackets my other side.

"Sorry, man. I didn't mean anything by it. Taylor's a cool chick, but I know she's taken." Jess hands me a bottled water in exchange for my beer.

I scrub my face and take the water. "I don't know what you're talking about."

Jess laughs. "Right."

"Just like you didn't shit a brick when she boarded the plane on the way to Rowdy's wedding," Gabriel casually throws out as he scans the backyard, probably looking for his woman.

Fuck. I thought I was stealthier than that. "Look—"

"Nope." Gabriel shakes his head, catching my eyes. "Not here. You need to talk, work out your frustrations at the gym, come find me. But not today, not like this. This is our family—your family. Respect that and keep yourself in check." He pats my back and ambles off.

"I'm not sure if that was a warning or if he was being supportive," I grumble as I watch him pull Frankie into a heated kiss, cupping her swollen belly where their second child is growing.

All this love every-fucking-where, rubbing my nose in it, is reminding me of my colossal failure in that department. It's hard to breathe. I rub my chest and finish off my water.

"Shit, I'm shocked he used so many words. But I'd say it's both. This is not the place to work out your shit."

I lose all rational thought when *she's* close. "Yep, I'm getting that."

"Come on, let's grab some grub. We can head out after if you're not feeling it."

We. Here I was ready to punch his face in, and he's being all amiable and shit. "Sounds good."

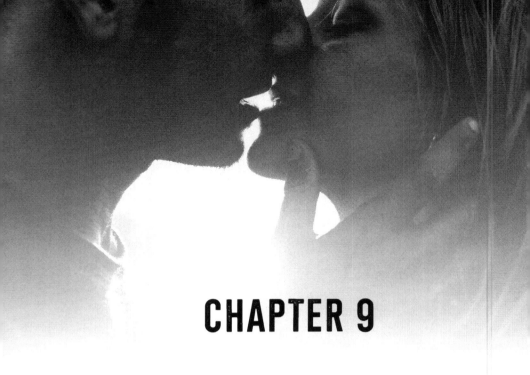

CHAPTER 9

'M ON MY SECOND PIECE OF DEATH BY CHOCOLATE cake—a girl has to drown her sorrows somehow, and alcohol is not my jam—when Cam plops down next to me, patting the rump of his ten-month-old son sleeping on his chest. His eyes slide to the bite I'm about to take. "Is that the last slice?"

I consider how much I love my brother, pulling the plate closer to my chest in case he's thinking of ripping it from my hands—wouldn't be the first time my food became a casualty of his hunger. "If I say yes, are you going to take it from me?" I shove the fork in my mouth, relishing every morsel of its silky, chocolaty goodness.

He directs my eyes to his son. "Kill's sleeping. I can't be fighting you for a piece of cake, but—"

"Here," I grumble as I hand him my plate. It's my second piece, anyway.

His dimpled smile is immediate and completely adorable. "Ah, Sis, really?"

I roll my eyes as if he didn't know what he's doing. "Don't get crumbs on my nephew's head." I stand to get another piece or something just as indulgent. "Save my spot."

A few moments later I've returned with a couple of waters and two slices of carrot cake. I glance at Cam as I sit. "Play your cards right, and one of these is yours."

"Damn, Tay, have I told you lately I'm happy you're here?" he says around his last bite of chocolate cake.

I pause, considering. "Actually, you haven't. Ever." I open a bottled water and hand it to him, not meeting his eyes. My emotions are still raw from my earlier encounter with Landry. I'm at a loss on how to fix it. Where to go from here. He obviously doesn't want anything to do with me. Should I quit? But I need—

"Hey. What's going on? I'm pretty sure I told you I was happy to see you when you first arrived. I wasn't blowing smoke up your ass."

"Little ears." Reese's shy smile reminds me how much I like her as she kisses Cam's cheek and sits on his knee.

"Kitten, he's asleep and can't even talk yet." His pout has her giggling and laying her head on his shoulder while placing her hand over Cam's on Killian's back. Cam's contented sigh has my empty heart fluttering with want and my gaze wandering around the party, only to lock on Landry's contemptuous stare from the other end of the patio.

"Here," I shove the uneaten pieces of carrot cake at Reese and Cam, "you want these?"

He frowns but takes them from me, handing one to Reese. "You sure? You just got them."

I stand, brushing down my shorts. "I'm sure." I've lost my appetite. I don't say that. I don't want them to think it has anything to do with their lovey-dovey display. It's heartwarming under any other circumstance, if only it weren't for the brooding man making me feel like I'm less than shit on the bottom of his shoes. "I need a bathroom break."

"Hey." Cam stops my retreat, gripping the tips of my fingers. "You sure you're okay?"

"Yep." I'm dandy.

"You don't want to talk about—"

"Nope. I'm good." I rush off before he can stop me or wring more emotions out of me. I'm not sure how he was going to finish that question, but I'm pretty sure it's a *no, I definitely do not want to talk.*

I go to the bathroom more to escape than use the facilities. When I come out, I wander around Cam's house. I've only been here one other time for a quick twenty-four-hour trip to meet my nephew Killian when he was born. I was too afraid to see Landry, and I had no idea Cap was my real father at that time.

Guilt chisels at my façade that all is A-okay. I've missed so much. Killian is ten months and barely knows who I am. I've tried to spend more time with them since I've arrived, but there's so much I'm not ready to talk about, and everywhere I turn, there's Cam, or Cap, or Landry, who are all part of the biggest can of worms I'm nowhere ready to open.

"Hey." Cam finds me in the upstairs game room rolling the eight ball along the emerald felt of his professional-size pool table.

I catch his gaze before looking away. "Hey."

His hands flex before he shoves them in his pockets.

What's got him on edge? I roll the ball hard enough for it to hit the opposite edge in front of him and bounce back to me.

"I was thinking it's time Cap tells the guys you're his daughter too. The longer we wait, the more awkward it'll be when they find out."

I still, squeeze my eyes closed and turn away. Landry has no idea. I'm nearly a hundred percent certain he hasn't figured it out. I don't even know if he knows I'm living with Cap and Cher. He never asked, and I didn't offer the information.

"What's going on?" Cam squeezes my arm, turning me to face him.

I blow a loose hair out of my face and shake my head. What the heck do I tell him? *I'm in love with your good friend and teammate, who hates me and had no idea I was your sister until your wedding, and he might just blow a gasket to know his boss is my father.* Yeah, no. "I need a minute." I dart around him for the stairs.

"Taylor," Rowdy calls after me.

"I need a minute, Cam." I don't stop. I dash down the stairs and into the kitchen, looking for Landry through the back windows before I exit. I stop abruptly when I find Landry and Cap sitting next to each other singing and playing their guitars.

Jesus, take the wheel. What am I going to do now? The good news is Cap is too busy to say anything, but that doesn't mean I can stop him or Cam without making a scene. I move closer, catching Cap's eye.

He lifts his chin, motioning to my guitar case to the right of Landry's feet. Does Cap want me to join them? If I do, can I control what happens next or just be closer to the explosion?

Cam comes barreling out the back door just as I step forward to open my case. I ignore my brother, keeping my head down, leaning in to Landry, whispering, "I need to talk to you." His chin dips, his brow furrows, but he doesn't look at me. "It's important."

I get a slight nod. I let out a breath, knowing he heard me.

I take the seat closest to Cap. I can see Landry better from here. I join in as they get to the chorus of "The Bones," surprised Cap even knows the song. I barely do.

One song leads into too many to count. At one point, it's just me and Cap playing James Taylor's "Shower The People." He starts, and I join in, getting lost in his voice and the emotions of singing my namesake's song, knowing Mom named me after James Taylor because of her and Cap's affinity for the singer, as well as Cap's first name being James. I'm Taylor Jamie instead of James, but it's close.

I can't look at Landry but practically feel his eyes boring a hole into my skull. When we finish playing, Cap closes his eyes, his head down. The deck is quiet. There are no claps and cheers like the other songs. They can feel it; the air is teeming with meaning.

My eyes ping to Landry, studying me like he's on the verge of figuring something out. I move to stand, needing to tell him. But Cap grabs my hand as he rises, setting his guitar in his seat. He looks at his family all around us, some related by blood, most not, and clears his throat.

Ohmygawd. This is where all hope dies. My gaze locks with Landry and holds as Cap finds his words.

"Y'all are family. Every damn one of you. I've been blessed with finding out Rowdy is my son, found love with Cher and blessed three times over with more children." He squeezes my hand, and my eyes fly to him. My watery gaze matches his. "But it was an added bonus to find out Taylor is my daughter too."

Everything around us erupts. Cher rushes in to hug her husband. Rowdy is at my side, pulling me into a hug. He kisses my temple, whispering, "See, that wasn't too bad."

I blink my tears away and look for Landry, but he's nowhere to be found. "Yeah."

CHAPTER 10

SHE'S CAP'S DAUGHTER! I CAN'T GET TO MY CAR fast enough. Thankful I parked on the street instead of being blocked in on Rowdy's driveway, I speed off, making a pit stop to buy a six-pack. It's not the same as drinking hard liquor like my dad... and his dad.

It's not the fucking same.

Arriving home, I drop my keys and empty my pockets on the table near the door. The silence itches up my spine. Mel's is closed, but for the first time in a long time, I wish it weren't. My phone rings. I pick it up. Jess. Decline call. It rings two more times before I turn it off, not even confirming if it's him or someone else.

I pop open a beer, placing the rest in my sparsely stocked fridge. Doesn't matter. I'm not hungry. Most my meals are eaten at Mel's or on the go with what I pack to take to Black Ops. I'm a bare necessities kinda guy.

I crash on the couch, kick my shoes off, and turn on Sports Center. When that doesn't keep my interest, I look for an action flick to occupy my mind. When none of that works, I go to grab my guitar, only to realize I left it at Rowdy's. In my haste to depart, I left her behind.

Finishing off my beer, I toss it and open another.

I'm two beers in, anger still simmering when there's a soft knock on my door. I jump because no one should be able to get to this door without going through the back door of Mel's. Fuck, did I leave it unlocked?

For half a second, I consider letting whoever is on the other side stand there until they give up and leave. Another knock, a little harder, but still too soft to be any of the guys.

Taylor. Did she run after me? I swing it open, ready to tell her *thanks, but no thanks,* only it's not Taylor.

"Ruby, what are you doing here? And how did you get in?"

She pushes past me. "I heard you might need some company tonight."

What the fuck? "Really? From who?" I scrub my face and turn toward her. I'm not nearly sober or drunk enough to deal with her.

"Walker." She shrugs, taking a look around. Her gaze lands on me, doing a once-over. "It's bigger than I thought."

Is she talking about my place or me?

"Not interested." I hold the door open, hoping she'll take the hint before I have to get meaner.

She eyes the beers on the coffee table. "You sure? I know you're my boss, but no one has to know."

I cross my arms. "The fact that I *am* your boss is exactly why you need to leave. It's not a line I'm willing to cross." *I'm not looking for a lawsuit when you realize I can never give you more than my dick.*

Said dick is asleep in my pants, not even a bit interested. He only has eyes for one girl, and Ruby isn't it.

"Then I quit." She bites her lip, sauntering over to run her finger down my arm.

She needs this job to help support her family. Her dad

disappeared on her mom and three sisters a few years ago. She attends college online.

"Still not interested." I soften my tone. "Look, Ruby, you're a catch with your looks and caring heart. But it's not in the cards for us."

Don't fuck this up by continuing to bark up the wrong tree. There's a whole fucking forest out there.

Her slow blinks and sad smile hit me harder than I anticipated. I don't want to hurt her, but I sure as shit don't want to lead her on. "Yeah," she nods, "I get it. Can't blame a girl for trying." She tips her chin, getting closer, giving me a chance to change my mind. "You sure?"

I pat her arm and step back. "I'm sure."

"Okay. Um, can I use your bathroom before I go?"

"First door on you right." I sigh and close the door. Apparently, this isn't going to be quick.

Not a minute passes with me walking the floor, counting steps till I can get back to wallowing in my beer, before there's another knock at the door. I don't hesitate, opening the door in a rush, ready to throw whoever the hell it is out.

Taylor jumps, screeching, wide eyes full of the tangled emotions that tighten my gut.

"Nope." Not doing this tonight. I slam the door shut in her face. Only her foot catches it.

"Ouch. Shit, Landry." She pushes it open with more strength than I would have expected from her. "Please, give me a minute." She holds up a case. "I brought your guitar."

My girl. I'm sorry I forgot you. I take the case from her and set it by the couch. *I'll be needing you later.*

"I'm really sorry—"

"Stop."

"But—"

"Just. Wait." I tower over her, trying to communicate with my eyes that we're not alone. I may not want to talk, but I definitely don't want to talk with Ruby in the next room. I don't need the whole damn bar knowing my business—Taylor's business.

"What…" Taylor trails off as the bathroom door opens, and she peers around me, her eyes bugging out.

Ruby stands there staring daggers at Taylor, then me when she notices our close proximity.

"You need a water for the road?" I ask, needing to let them both know Ruby is on her way out.

She seems to catch herself, regroups and pastes on a million-dollar smile that gets her all the guys—except me. "No, I'm good." She ambles over, ignoring Taylor, and leans up on her tip-toes, pressing a kiss to my cheek. "Thanks for tonight."

"Ruby," I growl. She's trying to start something she doesn't know anything about.

"Fine." She rolls her eyes, giving a curt nod to Taylor. "See y'all tomorrow." She closes the door behind her.

The air is tight and harder to come by now that the door is closed. "Hold on." I rush out the door slow enough to miss Ruby but fast enough to push the outer door closed and lock it. Stupid mistake for leaving it open. Hence the two unwelcome guests.

I punch out a breath of air, looking up the stairs to my open door. Maybe not all unwelcomed.

My seething anger has diminished, leaving disappointment and a knot in my insides warning me things are about to change.

She's my boss' daughter. I thought her being Rowdy's sister was bad enough.

"Taylor," I holler up the stairs.

She pokes her head out. "Yeah?"

"Why don't you come down? I'm going to make something to eat, and my fridge is empty." Eating is better than drinking my night away.

"Uh…" She glances into the apartment and back, "Okay," and closes the door before trotting down the stairs.

I head to the bar, grabbing a couple of sodas before entering the kitchen and switching on the lights, grill, and deep fryer. "Burger alright?"

"Sure." She pulls a stool over from the corner and sits opposite me at the prep table while I pull out ingredients.

"Mayo and mustard, no tomato, extra pickles and lettuce?"

"You remembered." The surprise in her voice reminds me of the cavernous void between where we were eight years ago and where we are now.

I sigh and stop myself from running my fingers through my hair, lock eyes with her and offer her my truth. "I remember everything, Songbird. There's not a moment or an inch of you I don't remember."

CHAPTER 11

I CAN HARDLY BREATHE, LOCKED IN LANDRY'S HEATED gaze. He's been so angry. I'd lost hope I'd ever get a glimpse of the boy I knew. I'm wholly thrown off by his honesty. I came ready to fight or beg him to listen, give me a chance to explain—apologize. I wasn't prepared to drop my walls and revel in echoes of our young love I've yet to find with anyone else or even want to experience again.

"I haven't forgotten," I whisper in the space between us that grows smaller by the second as my heart beats ever faster, thumping to find its other half.

He blinks. His back straightens. The moment is broken. He directs me on what to do with prepping the burger fixins as he grills the patties and cooks the fries.

I wallow in the reprieve, needing the time to regroup as we settle in the quiet peace of working side by side.

He may be mad, but he doesn't hate me. He wouldn't feed me if he hated me. He'd send me away like he did… "So, you and Ruby?" I leave the question hanging, not sure how to ask and pretty sure I don't want to know the answer. I ask anyway, digging in the wound that won't heal, pouring in salt and vinegar and lancing it just in case it's not painful enough.

"I'm a free man, Taylor. You left me a long time ago." There's no bite in his tone. He's stating fact, resolute in his certainty that I left him.

"I didn't leave you by choice," I whisper to his back as I slice a smallish tomato since he's the only one eating it. I can feel his eyes burning through the top of my head. "My older brother Drake showed up the morning I was supposed to meet you. He was angry I hadn't been returning his or my parents' calls. He literally dragged me to the car, threatening Cam to get our stuff and follow him as he drove me home. I never would have left you by choice."

I wanted to marry him. Play music. Swing on our front porch swing, sipping sweet tea while swatting at Texas-sized mosquitos. I wanted to have babies with him… lots and lots of babies.

I wanted to love him.

I wanted to be *loved* by him.

I wanted forever.

"Taylor." His gentleness hurts more than the memories.

"Don't coddle me, Landry. Yell at me, give me your anger, but don't be kind. I hurt you. I know. I recognize my part in failing you. But I honestly don't know how I could have done anything differently. I was powerless, overrun by my older brother and then my parents. They took my phone, my car, my computer, my ability to go anywhere except to school and home, and that was with Cam's supervision. He was forced to be my overlord, my jailer all because I fell for a boy they didn't know under his watch. I was wild, and they broke me."

"Jesus."

Yep. *Jesus, take the wheel.*

I'm broken in ways I can't even begin to tell him. In ways he will never be able to forgive me for.

Cam's a loose cannon when it comes to this topic. I'm afraid of what he'll do when he finds out Landry was the boy from spring break all those years ago.

I swipe at my tears and take a deep breath. I'm not a kid anymore. I'm twenty-three years old. I control my life. I won't let my past control my future.

I am in control.

"I'll quit," I throw out the only solution I know that puts distance between us, other than leaving Vegas, and I just can't seem to bear the idea of leaving him, Cam, Cap and everyone else who feels like the home I never had. "I don't want to cause you more heartache. I don't want to cause you trouble with Cap and your career. Though, I don't think he's the one you need to worry about. His vested interest is newer and not as deep-seated as Cameron's."

"I almost forget Rowdy's name is Cameron. You're the only one who calls him that." Landry slides the burgers onto the bottom bun.

I jump at his nearness, not realizing he's in my space, closer, yet still so far away. "It's weird to hear everyone call you Cowboy." I meet his hazel eyes. "I only know you as Landry. Cam talked about 'Cowboy' before his wedding, but I never suspected it could be you. Plus, I thought your dream was playing pro football."

His demeanor stiffens. "Yeah, I royally fucked that up."

There's a story there, but there's a story in everything we've barely scraped the surface of. It feels unattainable, like it could take a lifetime to work through the minutia of our relationship and life choices that brought us both to Vegas.

Our food ready, Landry grabs our plates. I follow with napkins, silverware, ketchup, and drinks. We slide into the nearest booth. Landry turns the jukebox on, playing low in the background.

"It's weird being here when the bar is empty." I stab a fry in ketchup.

His brow tips. "Bad weird?"

"Not bad, just different, like I'm not supposed to be here, or we're ghosts stuck at Mel's, living life just out of phase of everyone else, and we can't see them, but the place is packed."

His laugh is genuine, and his smile is soft and familiar. "I forgot you were a Trekkie."

"Not by choice, at least not initially. I was forced to watch it because my brothers liked it."

"I've heard about the house you grew up in. I can't imagine you not having a TV in your room, or another room where you could have watched whatever you wanted."

I shrug, cutting my massive burger in half. "I wanted to be near my brothers more than I wanted to avoid whatever Star Trek, Stargate series or movie was out at the time or on reruns."

A few bites in for me and half his burger gone, Landry wipes his mouth and hands, sitting back, pinning me with his gaze. "How long have you known Cap was your biological dad?"

"Thirteen days before I showed up at Cher's bakery." When I found out, I stuffed everything I could fit into my Maserati coupe and drove until I needed sleep, found a hotel and slept, continuing on the next day.

All was good, until it all went to shit in New Mexico right before I hit Arizona.

"Oh, yeah, I heard you just showed up with no warning. Were you trying to surprise them?"

"No, it was the only place I knew I could find."

He narrows his eyes. "What does that mean?"

"You didn't hear what happened?" I push my plate away, pulling my leg up under my other, and lean against the seat back.

"No. Tell me." He's nearly vibrating, ready to pounce at the first sight of trouble.

"I was robbed. He took everything I had except my duffel, guitar, and twenty dollars." I still can't believe he let me keep my bag and guitar.

"Did he hurt you?"

"He showed me I didn't know what the hell I was doing, and I suck in an emergency. It took me two weeks to get to Vegas. If it wasn't for a handful of kind souls, I don't know what would have happened to me." I swipe at a lone tear. I'm over crying about the past. "I'm sorry I didn't tell you about Cap, but they didn't know I knew until I arrived, and then Cher had the baby the same day. Things were crazy. Plus, it wasn't my secret to tell. This is his world. I don't have any right to come in here and make claims on him, his family, his business. I'm the outsider."

"You're family," he says with conviction.

"Maybe. I'm more like a guest in his life, in Cam's life. They're married, have babies." *What do they need with me?* "I'm just a visitor."

I don't belong in Texas. I don't really belong here, though I want to. I really, really want to.

"Taylor, you belong here."

Him believing that—more than I do—hurts. I miss the girl I used to be. I was confident. Certain of my place in the world.

Now, I'm certain I have no place.

I shrug, getting up. "I should go. Don't worry about Cap. He doesn't need to know anything." Landry didn't answer about me quitting. Do I still have a job?

He stops me just before I exit out the back. "How did you get here?"

"Jess brought me."

His scowl grows. "How are you getting home?"

I twist my lips. "He's waiting. He said he'll just sleep until I'm ready to go." Now that I say it out loud, I sound like a spoiled brat expecting him to sit out there waiting on me for hours. I really need to learn to use Uber. But I was desperate to get to Landry and explain. Good thing I didn't get here any sooner, or I would have interrupted him and Ruby. The thought sours my stomach.

I push through the door, unclear what will happen tomorrow, afraid he'll accept my offer to quit if I bring it up. Working at Mel's is the only contact we have.

"Taylor."

I turn, walking backwards. *Here it comes.*

He scratches his head, brow pinched. "I feel like I should say something... meaningful."

We learned some truths tonight. I'm not sure I can handle more. Yet I need to know. "Is this goodbye, or do I still have a job?" *Please, don't say goodbye.*

"It's *not* goodbye," he bites, stepping forward, then stops. "I expect to see you for your shift tomorrow."

Thank God. "Goodnight then."

"Night, Songbird."

A sad smile plays on my lips. He doesn't completely hate me if he didn't take the out I offered—to quit. But he never clarified if he's *with* Ruby. Tomorrow should be interesting. Maybe I'll be set loose and won't have to shadow her. It won't make working with her much better, but at least I won't be under her thumb as a trainee but as her equal.

Jess pops awake as soon as I open the passenger door. "Everything okay, Taytay?"

"Yeah." It could be better, but it could be way worse. "Thanks for waiting. Do you know how to Uber?"

He frowns. "You don't need Uber."

"I do if I don't want to rely on you or Walker to drive me around. I'm sorry you had to wait so long." When Landry offered to make food, I'd honestly forgotten Jess was waiting. I feel horrible. I should have just told him to leave and walk home.

Who am I kidding? These Neanderthals wouldn't have let me walk home, not Jess and certainly not Landry.

"Rely on me," Jess states like relying on others is easy.

It's not.

I sink into the seat as he pulls onto the road, leaving the man from my past behind.

CHAPTER 12

PAST ~ EIGHT YEARS AGO

PACE THE HOTEL LOBBY. CHECK MY WATCH. LOOK TO the elevator. Out front. Pace some more. Check my texts from last night.

Songbird: *I'll meet you in the lobby at 10a. I need a few hours of sleep, handsome. You wore me out.* 💋

Me: *Sleep when you're dead. Make it 9a. I want the whole day and night with you before we both head home.*

Songbird: *Okay, grumpy. Night. Love you!*

Me: *Love you more.*

Songbird: *Not possible.* 🖤

Damn, seeing her love in writing does something to me. But it's not enough to calm my worry. She's two hours late. I've called her, knocked on her door. The hotel won't tell me if she's checked out. She wasn't supposed to leave until tomorrow afternoon with her brother. I don't know what room he was in, or I'd be beating down his door.

I leave a note for her at the front desk, praying she'll get it, then head out to the beachfront to look for her or maybe her friends, but I'm pretty sure they were leaving this morning. It was supposed to be just the two of us staying in her room tonight. I should have stayed over last night, but I wanted her to enjoy her last night with her friends. Plus, as she said, we've been going at it pretty heavy. I don't think rabbits have a thing on us. If I'd stayed with her, her friends would have gotten quite a show no matter how sneaky or discreet we thought we were being. My girl is not quiet when she comes. They would have known.

Something is wrong. I just know it. It's a gut feeling.

I call her again, but it goes straight to voicemail like all the other times. I leave another message. I can't email her. We didn't exchange any other information. I don't even know her last name.

I decide to wait outside her room, ignoring the stares and remarks as guests walk past me. It's one o'clock by the time housekeeping shows up. The lady cleaning her room takes pity on me and lets me look inside.

Empty.

Her room is completely empty of any personal effects.

She's gone.

My Songbird flew the coop and didn't even bother to let me know. No goodbye. No fuck you very much.

Aimlessly, I make it back to my room, just in time to catch my friends getting ready to leave. Taylor and I were the only ones staying over an extra night because we couldn't bear the idea of leaving each other. She lives in Beaumont. I'm four and a half hours away in Dallas. It's not that far, but we're not neighbors either. Some states you can drive across in four hours. Not Texas. You can drive all day and never leave the state.

Everything is bigger in Texas, even my broken heart.

One of the guys drives my car home, while I bury my soul in liquor in the backseat. When we arrive in Dallas, I don't bother going home. I go to the nearest party and continue my Forget Taylor Exists plan. When it doesn't work, I drink till I pass out.

When I wake up, I puke, eat something, sometimes puke some more, then start drinking. On repeat. Day after day.

That's the extent of my senior year.

I not only fail out of high school, but I lose any hope of a college scholarship, NFL prospects, and nearly tear my throwing arm off when I crash into a tree.

Thankfully, the tree lived.

Sadly, so did I.

CHAPTER 13

T'S BEEN A FEW DAYS SINCE THE BIG *I'M CAP'S daughter* announcement. No one has treated me differently, except Landry. He's back to his distant, barely-notices-I'm-alive stance. I hang on to the fact that he didn't want to say goodbye. I gave him an out. He didn't take it.

But wanting something and making a move to have it are two totally different things.

Watching Ruby endlessly flirt with him is excruciating. It sickens me. I want to punch her. I guess that's further proof I am Cap's daughter—wanting to hit things when I'm upset. I'm practically part of the gym already.

I've taken to smiling bigger, laughing harder, killing them with kindness, and by them, I mean anyone who's not Landry. Him, I ignore. If I don't exist for him, he doesn't exist for me. It's a weird stalemate. But what choice do I have?

Go home?

Find another pub to work at?

Study and pass the Nevada bar exam?

Yep, none of those sit high on my list of wants. I'm lucky to be in a position to have a choice.

I still when I enter the kitchen and find Rowdy, Cap, and Cher sitting at the kitchen table full of breakfast like Cher's been cooking for hours.

Cher spots me first. "Good morning, honey. Gabriel cooked us breakfast. Won't you join us?"

She seems genuine. But Cam and Cap's matching scowls give me pause. Is this an intervention—but I'm not addicted to anything…? Maybe I should go for a run? Pack a bag and not come back? The thought sours my tummy.

"I…" I point over my shoulder and back away.

Jumping up, Rowdy moves quickly, gripping my wrist with a firm, "Sit."

"I'm not a dog." I wrench free and step back. "I have plans."

"Your plans can wait." He blocks my escape.

The only way out is through the back door. I consider it, but I don't have any shoes on, and my purse and phone are on the dresser in my room. I was only coming down for coffee to sip before getting ready to go to the bakery.

"Stop treating me like your *baby* sister. I'm grown. I don't need you bossing me around." I've had enough bossing for a lifetime, but with this bunch of overly sexed, testosterone-laden guys, I guess they think it comes with the territory.

Yeah, I don't want to think about my brother and father having sex lives, but they obviously do. They're spitting out babies left and right—Gabriel included. Frankie is pregnant again, and I've no doubt Cam is trying to knock up Reese as soon as possible to keep up with Gabriel. It's like a weird competition between them.

Cam steps closer, his shoulders lowering and his head bowing to meet my eyes. "Please come sit. We have some things to discuss."

Giving him the stink-eye, I shove him and move past him to the table. "You could have just said that."

"I did." He trails behind me.

"No. You ordered me to sit. *Cher* asked nicely."

When we're both seated, I glance to a smiling Cap and offer, "Good morning," to him and Cher.

"Morning, Taylor." He's nearly laughing.

"Don't look so pleased, Cap. She's a brat." Rowdy places a cinnamon roll on my plate before loading it with an egg casserole concoction, potato hash, and bacon.

Cher laughs over her cup of coffee, her one indulgent cup a day since she's nursing.

"It's nice to hear your banter, acting like normal kids."

"We're not kids," Cam and I reply in harmony.

That has Cap chuckling. "Right. Okay. Siblings. That better?"

"Yes."

"Barely," I grumble. I love my brother, but, hello, give me some space to breathe and find my way in life.

Though I guess he has. He's been gone for years. I had to learn to grow up without him. Graduated from high school and college without him. Lost Mom... without him. I set my fork down and close my eyes.

Mom, I miss you. I'm angry at you, but miss you all the same.

Cap squeezes my hand, drawing my eyes to him. "Did your mom ever tell you how she got her name?"

My eyes fly to Cher. She only waves me off. "I don't mind you talking about your mother. In fact, I want you to. She was a big part of all of your lives. It's okay to remember her, talk about her, say her name in everyday conversation. I don't mind, honestly."

Cap kisses her cheek on a gruff, "Plum." It's only her nickname, but it puts color on her cheeks and has him looking like he wants to devour her.

These guys are sexed up to the hilt.

"About Mom's name?" Cam brings us back to the question at hand.

I fork a bite of food and decide I can probably stomach a bit more.

Cap takes a deep drink of his coffee and sets it down. "Her parents couldn't decide on her name. Her father wanted to call her Lena. Her mom wanted to call her Vera. It wasn't until your mom was a few days old that they finally came to an agreement—a compromise. They named her Vera Orlena."

"Yeah, we know." Cam frowns, trying to figure what the big deal is.

I laugh when it hits me. "Oh my god, I never knew that!"

"What?!" Cam looks between us.

Cher seems lost too.

I nod to Cap to clarify for them. "They named her Vera OR-lena." He laughs. "I always thought that was the funniest, quirkiest thing I'd ever heard about a name. I can't imagine putting an *or* in my kid's name just because we couldn't agree."

"It's actually kinda clever." I unwrap my cinnamon roll, taking a big bite, trying not to moan over its warm, gooey, sugary goodness.

Cap's hand is over mine again, but this time it stays. "I was young when I loved your mom. Too young to be the man she needed. But I'm forever grateful to her for giving me you, Taylor."

Oh, crap. Cue the tears.

"And you, Cameron. I'm one lucky guy to have two great kids to call my own and help me—" he looks to Cher, "—us raise our little brood. It's a second chance to do it right, but don't think for a moment that I love you two any less."

Now I'm full-on sobbing, pulled into a sitting Cap hug with my brother plastered to my back, and I reach for Cher's hand over the table. "I love y'all," I manage through shaky emotions and a matching voice.

"I love you too, Taylor and Cameron, and my Plum." Cap's emotion-riddled voice vibrates in my ear.

"Love, y'all," from Cam.

After a few minutes, we sit back down, wiping at our eyes, laughing at our emotions and the silliness that brought about Mom's name. I wonder why she never told us that.

There are so many things she never told us.

"Is that why we're here?" I can't imagine Rowdy is here to hear this story about Mom or for Cap to share his feelings.

"No," Cam speaks up. "Dad called." He flashes to Cap before coming back to me. "Barrett."

Yeah, I knew who he meant, but it *can* be confusing. "And?"

"The cops found your car and thief."

Dots dance in my vision.

They found him.

I can't breathe.

"Whoa. Put your head between your legs." Cam pulls out my chair and forces my head down.

"Breathe, Taylor," Cap encourages.

They found him.

They found him.

They found him.

The tears keep coming. The air gets thinner and harder and harder to come by.

CHAPTER 14

JAKE HANGS UP THE PHONE BEHIND THE BAR AS I pass. "Taylor's coming, but she'll be late." He goes back to stocking the glasses.

"How late?" I study him like he's withholding details.

"She didn't say, but she sounded upset, not sick." He shrugs, turning away.

Why didn't she call *me*?

As I remember I never gave her my number, my phone vibrates in my pocket with an incoming call. Rowdy. It can't be a coincidence. "Hey. Are you calling about Taylor?"

"Yeah. Can you let me in?"

"In?"

"I'm at the entrance of Mel's." He ends the call before I can ask why the hell he's here a little before five o'clock in the afternoon when he should be home with his wife and kid. He has been known to come out occasionally, but never at this time of day and never alone.

I push the door open, squinting at the Vegas sun as it tries to bleed into Mel's bar. "What are you doing here?"

He motions past me. "Let me in, and I'll explain."

I move aside and let him pass, pulling the door closed till it clicks. Arms folded, I wait when all I really want to do is press forward until he breaks and tells me what's wrong. He's giving off all kinds of weird vibes, and it's making me itch.

"Taylor can't make her shift. I'm here to cover for her." He's serious.

"What's wrong with Taylor? She called and said she'd be late."

He's shaking his head before I even finish. "No, she's not coming. But this job is important to her, and she doesn't want to leave you in the lurch." He presses on before I can tell him to go home. "I know I'm not her. I'm not trained, but I can do anything you need me to do if you don't want me to serve. I'm here. Put me to work, Boss."

I laugh. I don't like not knowing what's going on with Taylor, but I can see he's determined. It's almost like he needs something to do. We can survive being down a server, so Taylor missing a shift isn't the end of the world. It won't be the first time we've been short...

On the other hand... Maybe if I let him stay, he'll open up about what's going on. "You can help Jake at the bar. You can't make drinks, but you can help keep it stocked, run food, drinks, clear tables, and if Walker ends up short a guy, you can be a bouncer. I'll cover the tables Taylor would have had."

"Cap is going to come later and take her gig if you're okay with an old dude singing."

Yeah, like I'd turn down my boss and their father. "He's talented. He might class up the joint."

"And by class up, you mean start a brawl."

"Exactly."

I put Rowdy to work, leaving him in the capable hands of Jake. If need be, Walker can take over the bar with Jake—a certified mixologist— and put Rowdy on covering the door.

That's what I end up doing two hours later when we get slammed right before Taylor is scheduled to go on. She's becoming more popular each time she sings. I swear half these guys are here specifically to see her, and it rubs me the wrong way.

A few minutes before seven, I spot Taylor rushing in through the back door, slipping into the employee lounge. I signal Jake. "I'll be right back."

Her back is to me when I enter. "You okay?" My heart pounds in anticipation of her answer. She's been off since Rowdy's cookout when I found out she was Cap's daughter, I admitted I remember every inch of her, and she confessed she didn't leave me by choice. All of it was hard to hear, and imagine how alone she felt, having no control over her life. My life was out of control, and I blamed her. *Blamed*. It's been eight years.

A part of me says it's best to leave what we had in the past and move on—without her, regardless of the reason she left. There's no reason to dredge it all up and risk the wrath of Cap and Rowdy. Then there's the other half of me that wants to sweep her in my arms and hold her until she remembers she belongs to me—always has and always will.

It's a battle I'm sure to lose either way.

"Yep. I'm sorry I'm late." She snaps her guitar case closed and turns.

My breath catches. She's a stunner in her tight jeans and off-the-shoulder top. She's not wearing her Mel's Bar t-shirt like she usually does. I guess missing her shift helped with more flexible clothing options. But her eyes tell another story of why she was late tonight. One of sadness and… brokenness.

I step forward, stopping just short of pulling her into my arms. "What happened?"

She shakes her head. "I know I owe you an explanation. But if you want me to perform, and if I have any hope of making it onto that stage, you can't ask me that right now. I'm barely hanging on."

I nod and move aside. Before she makes it to the door, I swallow my pride and give her something she may need but not want. "You look beautiful, Songbird."

Her forehead hits the door. "Landry." It's a merciful plea.

I place my hand above her head on the door, ensuring no one tries to open it and knock her over in the process. It's also an excuse to get closer.

"You don't have to go on if you're not up for it. You can go home. Come back when you're settled."

"No coddling, remember?" She leans back, the warmth of her strikingly familiar even after all these years.

I want to wrap myself in her, forget about our past and whatever has her upset today. I want to be what she needs. I run the tips of my fingers along the curve of her neck, breathing in her warm, floral scent. "There's much I want to do to you, Taylor, but coddling isn't one of them." A total lie, pampering her is exactly what a part of me wants to do, the part that wants to forgive and move forward... together.

She shivers on a faltering inhale. "I need to go to work."

I step back, giving her room to leave, giving my body a moment to calm down, stop it from following and tackling my Heartbreaker to the floor.

After a handful of minutes, I stride out, catching Rowdy's gaze as Taylor steps up to the mic among whoops, cat calls, and whistles.

Fuckers treating her like a stripper instead of a musician.

I want to tell them all she's more amazing than they can imagine, and she's mine. They don't even have the right to look at her.

The reality that she is, in fact, not mine burns and twists in my gut, cracking my heart I've worked hard to barricade from further assaults.

But if she didn't leave by choice...

"When did she get here?" Rowdy stands wide, arms across his chest looking like the menace he's capable of unleashing. He's not crazy about the attention she's drawing either.

"A few minutes ago." My attention drifts back to the stage as Taylor starts the intro to "You and I," but it's not the Lady Gaga arrangement. It's slower, grittier... sultrier.

"Fuck." He runs a hand over his jaw. "She's incredible, but these fuckers—"

"Think she's ripe for the picking," I add, not helping his agitation nor mine one bit.

"Yeah." He cracks his neck. "Not sure I can stand here without knocking someone the fuck out. Can't believe she thought she could *walk home* after shifts."

I chuckle darkly, feeling the same but not voicing it. I actually relax knowing he'd demolish the room to protect her.

Then he has to go and ruin my calm when he confides in me why she was late.

I'm dumbstruck and pissed off all at the same time. She has to identify the guy who robbed her. "When does she go?"

"Tomorrow. Cap is going to take her in the morning. She doesn't want me to go. Says I'm too much of a loose cannon."

"Is she wrong?"

"No. Dammit." He's not happy about it. He eyes me, working something out in his head. "You like her."

Shit. I fight the need to puff out my chest and tell him I'm proud she's mine, not ashamed or disrespecting her, but... She's *not* mine. "Yeah, she's great. What's not to like?"

He narrows his eyes. "You know that's not what I'm saying."

"She's your sister." *And my employee, and my ex—though you have no idea about that.*

He gives me a chin lift and turns back to the stage. "I'd be okay with it."

There's a whoosh in my ears as my mind settles on what he's saying. Is he giving me permission? "Are you trying to tell me something?"

"I just did." He eyes me over his shoulder and moves closer to the stage.

Well, that's an unexpected turn of events.

His words resonate, planting like hope in my heart.

I text Cap.

Me: *I'm coming with you tomorrow.*

The text shows read almost immediately, and three dots bounce as he types his reply.

Cap: *Happy to have you. Be here at 8 sharp.*

I've no idea what I'm doing, but I think the part of me that wants to forgive is winning out. My gut is telling me to be cautious.

She's not the same girl you knew.

You're not the same naive kid you were at seventeen.

She trampled your heart, threw you away like yesterday's trash.

Or did she?

CHAPTER 15

I DIDN'T THINK I'D GET ANY SLEEP, BUT APPARENTLY, I did. Singing is cathartic. I went to work because it was an obligation, but also because I needed it. I sang my heart out, gritty, seductive, loud, angry, contemptuous, soft, heartbroken—all of it wrapped in melody and words. I live, grieve, love, die, and regenerate in songs.

I am a phoenix—reborn.

Laughing at my silly, reflective thoughts, I grab my purse and head downstairs to the kitchen, pausing at the downstairs guest room when I spot Cher nursing Iris.

She waves me in. "Morning, honey."

"Good morning." I take her outstretched hand, giving it a squeeze as I run my other hand over Iris' magically soft hair. It's like silk and rose petals and smells like heaven. "You need anything?" I direct to Cher.

"No. I'm good." She eyes my purse. "You doing okay?"

"I'm good."

Her sympathetic smile has my nerves ramping up. *I don't want to do this.*

"I know a thing or two about bad men. You need to talk, I'm here.

Or, if you need to sit and not talk, I'm here for that too. I wish I could go with you."

"No, you don't." I laugh. Nobody wants to go to the police station, especially her. From the highlights I know of Cher's past, she dislikes hospitals and police stations.

"Okay, maybe it's more accurate to say I wish I was there to support you."

"You already are." She's been nothing but nice and accepting of me since I arrived nearly two months ago. She has a full house of babies and the man she loves, yet I've never felt unwelcomed or like an outlier beyond the insecurities in my head.

"Your father is in the kitchen, worrying about you. He may need you more than you need him today." She squeezes my hand in parting, encouraging me to eat something before we go.

I nearly swallow my tongue when I find Cap, Cam, and Landry in the kitchen drinking coffee and laughing. I can understand why Cam is here. But Landry? My senses go on alert. Though, I'm pretty darn sure they wouldn't be laughing if they knew about my past with him. He must be here for another reason.

My brother spots me first. "Tay, come eat." Always with the orders.

Landry smirks, seemingly the only one who notices my frown. "What he means is, breakfast is on the table if you'd like some."

Better. Leave it to Landry to smooth things over with gentle words. He's a peacemaker. He must be a middle child. I try to remember if has siblings. We didn't talk about our families much when we—

"Morning, Taylor. Coffee?" Cap pops up, heading to the coffee machine.

"Good morning, and yeah, I'd love a cup." I eye the table with what looks like the fixins for taquitos: eggs, sausage, bacon, cheese, jalapenos, sour cream, salsa, homestyle hashbrowns, and the tortilla warmer. "Someone got up early to do all this."

"Reese made it for me to bring over." Cam points to the seat next to

Landry. "There's a place setting ready for you." He glances at Landry and back to me. "If you want it."

"It looks good." I slide into the seat. Landry places a glass of orange juice next to my plate. For a moment I wonder if it's spiked. I need that more than the food.

The guys get back to talking shop while I fill my plate. From what I can gather, Landry has a fight coming up. Something about another guy dropping out, and Cap was able to secure Landry a spot.

Before I get halfway through my first taquito, Gabriel waltzes in with a cooler in one hand and Maddox in his arms. "Mornin'." His morning-gruff greeting has his son's eyes skating around the room, then his head buries in his daddy's neck. "Someone's not awake just yet." He kisses Maddox's head.

"I know the feeling, Maddox. I wouldn't mind going back to sleep myself." I greet him with a small smile. As a reward, Gabriel plops Maddox in my lap, who instantly lays his head on my shoulder. I hug him, relishing the warm and calm it gives me to hold another person. I guess I needed a hug too.

When I get back to the business of eating, Maddox ends up devouring most of my taquito. Landry silently sets another one on my plate and dishes up more potatoes to replace those Maddox gobbled down like they were the best food ever, which, they are pretty darn good. Maddox doesn't say anything, just nods, shy smiles and wide eyes. He's going to be the strong silent type like his daddy with expressive blue eyes that'll get him whatever he wants. Unable to resist, I kiss his forehead.

He surprises me by clamping his hands on my face, bringing my head down and kissing my forehead, then he plucks a handful of potatoes and shoves them in his mouth.

Stunned, I glance up into the laughing eyes of his father. "He just started doing that to Frankie. My little man trying to be all grown up, copying his daddy."

"There are worse things he could emulate." I shrug and wipe Maddox's mouth, wanting to kiss the bundle of heart in my lap again.

Gabriel and the guys finish up what's left of the food but not before I confirm Cher has eaten. Cap gives me a warm smile, reassuring, "I fed her first." Of course he did.

At some point Maddox falls asleep with his head against my breast. Gabriel checks that I'm okay to hold his son before going to say hi to his mom. I manage to slide Maddox higher as I leave the kitchen and seek out the glider recliner in the living room. It's the best seat in the house, in my opinion, but with Cher nursing, I don't sit in it unless Iris is with me. Today, Maddox affords me the luxury. I sink into its plush cushions and gently glide back and forth, closing my eyes and dwelling in the peaceful sanctuary of another life taking comfort in my arms.

I don't let my mind drift to where it always wants to go when I hold a baby or, in this case, a large toddler. Maddox will be three in a few months, but he's bigger than most kids his age, which is no surprise given who his daddy is.

A tender touch to my cheek has my eyes popping open to a frowning Landry. He skims under both eyes. "Why are you crying, Songbird?"

I'm crying for things you can never know and a future that'll never be.

His stare only intensifies when I don't look away. He bends and kisses my cheek, whispering, "You'll tell me all about it when you're ready."

I'll never be ready.

You'll never want to hear this.

My hand slides down his cheek as he pulls away.

Everyone stops at the entrance of the living room, staring at us, me in the glider with a sleeping Maddox and Landry at my side, his hand on my shoulder. Questions dance in each of their eyes. Cap holds my twin brothers, one in each arm: Cade and Wade, Cher with a sleeping Iris, Cam studying us intently holding the cooler Gabriel brought, and then there's a smiling Gabriel, his focus on his son resting soundly. I have a feeling not much fazes him.

"Are y'all ready?" I never quite gathered why everyone was here today. Most days it's just me with Cap and Cher's family, though, I guess, staring at everyone in the doorway, they are their family.

"Yep," Caps speaks first, heading out the front door with the twins, diaper bag over his shoulder bouncing against his back as he walks.

"Here." Landry offers his hand, pulling me up without waking Maddox.

"You okay to carry him?" Gabriel asks as I near.

"Yeah, but I don't think I can get him in his car seat without waking him."

"I'll take him once we're outside. No reason to jostle him twice." He scans me. "You need a purse or something?"

"Oh, yeah. I'll—"

"Got it." Landry heads back inside, coming back with my purse in hand. I'm stunned he even noticed where I placed it. Most guys don't notice that stuff, do they?

I slow as we pass Cam's truck, with him leaning in the back door on one side and Cap doing the same on the other. They're putting the twins in their car seats. I guess they're going to the gym daycare with Cam since Cap is coming with me. So now I know why Cam was here.

Gabriel lifts Maddox from my arms with ease, placing him in his car seat in the back of his Hummer without waking him. He eases the door closed with barely a click and surprises me with an unexpected hug. "Good luck today. You need anything, let me or Frankie know."

"Thanks." I end the hug first, not sure how to take all this protectiveness from these guys. Was Gabriel only here to lend support?

Cam hugs me quickly with sad eyes. He's unhappy he's not coming with me, but I think it's for the best. I need to stay as emotionless as possible, and I can't do that with Cam there. He knows me too well not to see through my *I'm okay* façade. He'll want to dig in places I'd rather he didn't, and I'm not sure I have the energy to hold the wall steady, knowing he'll be hurt by keeping him at arm's length, as well as Cap and Landry.

When Cam and Gabriel drive off, it's just Cap, Landry and me. Cap looks to me. "Ready?"

"As I'll ever be."

Landry opens the back door of Cap's Escalade. "After you."

"I'm sorry, what?"

Cap chuckles under his breath, placing the cooler Gabriel brought on the passenger side floorboard and closing the door before rounding the front to the driver's side.

"I'm coming with you." Landry waves me in like I don't understand the concept of getting inside a car.

"I don't—"

He crowds me. "I'm. Coming. With. You," he growls in my ear, punctuating his words with a squeeze to my waist, then he lifts me into the back seat when I can't do anything but breathe through his closeness and relish the protectiveness in his words and demeanor. It gives me hope I have no business feeling.

He's the king of mixed signals. At the moment he's running hot, but I've no doubt as soon as I let my guard down, he'll run cold, ignoring me again, freezing me out.

A girl could catch pneumonia in this climate.

CHAPTER 16

THE CLOSER WE GET TO FLAGSTAFF, WHERE THE guy caught driving her car was arrested, the more Taylor's agitation grows. She's noncommunicative, sticking to her side of the back seat, eyes trained on the passing view of the dry but beautiful terrain. I sat back here with her thinking she might want the support without having to ask—she always hated being vulnerable and putting herself out there. But I was mistaken. I haven't earned that right. I placed her in the seat when she looked about to panic, trying to figure out my game. I have no game other than supporting her through something that's obviously upsetting.

Not offering her the choice of seats was a mistake that stressed her out more. It's hard to remember she's not mine. In some ways she looks exactly like the girl I fell in love with—the one who liked my assertive ways. Then, other times, she's a complete stranger. It's a line I'm having trouble navigating.

When we make a pit stop about halfway there, I switch to the front seat, giving her the space she seems to need. Cap and I share glances, but neither of us tries to draw her into conversation after unsuccessfully attempting for the first hour.

After a bite to eat from the lunch Gabriel packed, which was grilled chicken Caesar salad with crisp veggies wrapped in spinach tortillas, and cups of fresh berry yogurt parfait with granola, she put in her earbuds and lay down across the backseat. Cap and I both took a collective sigh in relief to see her settle down, and the palpable buzzing in the air eased.

"I think something happened beyond her getting robbed," I admit when I'm sure she's asleep with music playing in her ears. "She hasn't been herself since she arrived."

His gaze slides my direction before returning to the road ahead. "I don't disagree, but I'm curious. Seems you two know each other better than you're letting on."

"I don't know what you're talking about."

"Not buying it."

"That's not the point of this conversation," I redirect, hoping he'll let it go.

He chuckles at my deflection. "No, I suppose it's not. But I think *that* conversation needs to be had at some point."

"Noted."

"Why do you think there's more going on than her being robbed?" He motions to the sign denoting Flagstaff is thirty-five miles ahead.

"She's too nervous, on edge about it. Didn't she have a panic attack when she found out the police had the guy in custody yesterday?"

"Yeah, I guess she did." He considers it for a moment. "I just assumed it was the reminder of how helpless she felt and the challenging task of making her way to Vegas without money or means for food or transportation."

"That's off too. Why wouldn't she have used someone's phone to call her dad?" Oh, shit. "Sorry, I mean—"

"Barrett." He waves me off. "It's okay. He's still her dad. He raised her."

Okay then. "She could have called Rowdy or you. Anyone answering the phone at the Black Ops Gym would have hopped in a car to help her, sent her money, a new cell phone, a plane ticket... anything for Rowdy's sister. I don't buy that it didn't cross her mind. She's not that easily flustered or irresponsible. Something happened to make her feel like she *couldn't* reach out for help."

"Damn. Why didn't I consider that?" He scrubs his face. "She didn't want Rowdy to come because he'd know something was wrong. He knows her too well." He eyes me again as we slow, coming into a town just outside of our destination. "Which brings me back to my point earlier. Before she started working for you, you two never hung out. Yet you know her better than having just met at Rowdy's wedding. I don't remember you hanging out there either."

"You were probably too busy ogling your soon-to-be wife to pay attention."

"Nope. It was the first time seeing Taylor after finding out she was mine. I watched you two *not* watch each other. I didn't really understand it then. But now I know it means you knew her from before, and I'm betting Rowdy doesn't know."

I chuckle at the craziness of the situation. "*I* didn't know."

He nods, comprehension settling over him. "I don't think he'd mind."

I shake my head on a sad laugh. "Believe me, he will—*you* will."

"Why don't you try me?"

Keeping my gaze out the side window, I catch Taylor's reflection, her eyes closed, still sleeping. I've said too much already. "It's not my story to tell." The same words she gave me about Cap being her true father. It was Cap's secret to reveal. My relationship with Taylor is hers to convey to her family when and if she's ready. I have a vested interest in the telling, but it's not my place to reveal what she obviously doesn't want known.

She pretended I didn't exist at Rowdy's wedding. I asked her to continue that façade once she started working for me. There was no reason to rock the boat for a history long gone and we had no intention of repeating.

Now, things are twisted, and she's deep in the middle of something that happened on her way to Vegas, and none of us know what it is or how to help her. I don't want to pretend I don't know her. That I don't know her better than Cap and maybe even Rowdy. I want her to belong to me despite my blackened heart telling me to shut the fuck up, stay the course. Leave history where it belongs—in the past.

I can't deny the hurt in her eyes. It's greater than our history, may not even have anything to do with it. She's going through something, and even if I didn't know her better than anyone else realizes, I'd still want to help. She's Rowdy's sister, Cap's daughter. They're my family too, making her family.

But, damn, I can't deny I want her to be more than shared responsibility or family by association. I want her in every conceivable way, despite our past, her current trauma, and quite possibly at the risk of losing my MMA career and family by choice if they reject me as not good enough for her.

If I had to choose, I'm pretty sure I'd pick Taylor every damn time.

The stop and go and turning me has me popping awake, sitting up to what looks like an old-time downtown through the car windows. I pull out my earbuds. "Are we here?" I yawn and stretch, checking the time on the dash. We made pretty good time, a little more than four hours.

"Yes. You need to stop before we go to the police station?" Cap's green eyes that match my own flash in the rearview mirror.

I catch sight of a donut shop ahead. "Maybe a coffee and a donut."

Or a dozen. I love Cher's sweets, but I'm a sucker for donuts, all kinds, but bear claws, to be sure, are my downfall.

Landry expressive hazel eyes meet mine over his shoulder. "You want me to go in and grab food, or you want to have a seat and drink your coffee?"

"I could use the bathroom too. Stretch my legs."

"Going in it is." Cap pulls into the closest parking spot. I set my purse on the floorboard and pocket my phone before climbing out with the assistance of Cap's extended hand.

Inside, I spy the only donuts that can make this day bearable.

Landry leans in, staring at the menagerie of sugary goodness. "I'll order while you visit the ladies."

I point out what I want, mourn over the twelve others I'd like to try and head to the restroom.

When I return, I find Cap and Landry sitting at a booth, munching on donuts. I debate for two seconds who to sit by then slide in next to Landry. It feels weird to not choose his side, especially since the extra coffee and plate are sitting next to him, like it's waiting on me. I'd be making an unnecessary point to sit by Cap and slide the coffee and plate to that side. I don't want to alienate Landry any more than I already have.

A box of donuts and another with warm kolaches rest on the middle of the table. I dig into my bear claw, pulling off a finger at a time, relishing the sugary goodness as it coats my tongue with its warmth and tender dough before melting in my mouth. I could eat myself into a sugar coma before I'd tire of warm, fresh, fried dough. The sweetness is only broken up by bites of mini sausages wrapped in more dough.

"Thank God Cher doesn't make donuts too. I'd eat my weight in them every day." Not that I don't consume entirely too many of her sweets and warm breads as it is.

"Donuts are your jam?" Landry asks, biting what looks to be a chocolate Bavarian crème-filled bar, with an apple fritter waiting on deck.

"Donuts are my kryptonite." I lick my lips and fingers, not wanting a single sugary flake to be missed.

Cap laughs around a simple glazed with two more on his plate with a chocolate iced chaser.

Stuffed with two bear claws and two kolaches, I refill my coffee as Cap and Landry decide on waters for the road. In the Escalade, I respond to a text from Cam, letting him know we made it and are heading to the police station. The reality of that text sits like a dead weight in my stomach. Maybe eating wasn't such a great idea. But donuts...

At the police station, I follow Cap through the double doors and come to a halt just inside, making Landry grip my hips to stop from smashing into my backside. I lean back, wanting to backtrack.

I can't do this.

"Hey, you got this." Landry's soft encouragement and gentle nudge force me forward.

Cap does most of the talking until the detective in charge of my case finds me in the waiting area. "Detective Bryant," he offers like I should recognize his name. "I spoke to your brother, Cameron, yesterday." He shakes my hand before doing the same to Cap and Landry. "Why don't you come this way?"

He shows us into a fishbowl conference room, windows on the outside and on all the interior walls. I'm not sure if it's meant to intimidate: *you can't hide from me,* or more *you're welcome in our inner sanctum.* Either way, it's unnerving.

I snatch Landry's water and chug half of it, giving him an *I'm sorry I need this more than you do* look.

"I appreciate you driving down here on such short notice. But I figure you'd probably want to get your car back as soon as possible."

Yeah, no. "I couldn't care less about the car. It'll go back to Texas when you're done with it." Dad—Barrett—can sell it, burn it, crush it for all I care. I did love that car, but not anymore. All it did was bring me unwanted attention. I never would have run into Beau Montana or whatever his real name is if it weren't for that flashy car.

"Really? It's a sweet ride. There's no damage as far as I can tell."

Oh, there's damage alright. You might not be able to see it, but—

"Let's table what happens to the car for now," Cap interjects, saving me from the rant in my head. "What do you need from Taylor?"

"I need to get your statement, identify your car, and look at a line-up to see if you find your perp." Det. Bryant makes it sound so easy, like it's a shopping list. A checklist: one, two, three.

I squeeze my hands in my lap, glancing between Cap and Landry sitting on either side of me and back to Det. Bryant. "Which do we do first?"

He squints, noticing my reaction. "Gentlemen, I'll need you to step outside while I conduct the interview."

CHAPTER 17

GRUMBLING, WE EXIT THE INTERVIEW ROOM, WITH me wanting to protest the entire time. Taylor wouldn't look at us as we left. Something is most definitely up.

"She doesn't want to keep her car?" I question as soon as we're sitting on the other side of the glassed-in room. "Do you know what kind it is?"

"It's a Maserati MC20 Coupe."

I whistle. "That's some major chunk of change." I google it just to confirm. Yep, it costs more than my childhood home. But I hear she grew up in a McMansion, so a Maserati's price tag is a drop in the bucket when your family is worth billions.

"Why wouldn't she want to keep it, at least to resell it?" Anger simmers just below the surface. I'm not sure I can deal with knowing some guy hurt her. The fact that he stole from her and left her stranded is bad enough.

"I don't know. On top of the trauma, knowing the asshole drove her car all this time after robbing her is enough I probably wouldn't want it back either, if I were in her shoes. Honestly, I'm surprised it didn't end up in a chop shop."

I blink hard between the piece of paper before me and over my shoulder at Cap and Landry's backs. "Will they know?"

"No. It's an ongoing investigation. No one outside of the force will know the details unless you share them." He leans forward, sincerity in his eyes and manner. "But I encourage you to talk to someone. You shouldn't have to deal with this on your own."

"And after this, if I identify him, what will happen?"

"If you press charges, he'll be detained, and it's up to the DA if they move forward with prosecution if we don't get an admission of guilt." He pauses, tapping on the printout of my statement. "This could be hard to prove, given the circumstances and no physical proof."

"His word against mine."

"Unfortunately.

"Then why report it at all?"

"Because there's a chance, Taylor, he could be charged with more than just larceny and grand theft auto. What does it hurt to try?"

"Me." My chin trembles, and I look away, ashamed of how I handled this whole situation. "It hurts me."

He sits back, arms resting wide on the table. "I understand. You want to think about it?"

The last thing I want to do is *think* about it—about *him*. "I don't want it to happen to anyone else."

"Then sign the paper, Taylor, and let's get this scumbag off the streets."

Det. Bryant lets us accompany Taylor into an observation room where we're hidden behind one-way glass. Hopefully she can identify the thief. With me on one side and Cap on the other, Taylor grips my hand and steps back when the guys start filing in.

The detective has each of the five suspects step forward, turn to the side, then forward again before having them step back in line. Each time Taylor shakes her head, defeat riddling her body.

He's not here. I scrutinize each of the guys, like I know what he looks like, like I can see the evil that would dare to steal from Taylor.

The cop sighs and calls the next guy until there are no more.

Dejected, Taylor wrings her hands, then wraps them around herself, still staring through the window, finally confirming what her head shakes mean. "He's not in there."

Det. Bryant lets out a punch of air. "I was afraid of that. The man we caught driving your car said he wasn't the one who stole it originally. He took it off some drunk guy in a bar a few nights go—or so he says. I couldn't be sure until you confirmed he's not your assailant."

Assailant? That sounds way more dramatic than thief. I eye Cap, and his scowl confirms he didn't miss the word choice either. He wraps his arm around his paling daughter. He's not looking much better.

"I'd like to have you look at some mugshots to see if you spot the guy." When the detective ushers them out of the room, I have the distinct urge to maim someone—a specific thieving someone.

On shaky legs, I follow the detective to my car. I don't imagine there are too many Maseratis in Flagstaff. Not because people can't afford one, but it just seems more like an outdoorsy kinda place, and a Maserati doesn't scream *I like to hike and go camping.* I could be wrong, but I do know my

Maserati is the only one in the police impound lot. I spot her immediately, noting she's in need of a good washing. Her gunmetal gray exterior is caked with dirt.

"Did the guy go mudding or something?" Landry circles the car with obvious appreciation.

She is a beauty when she's clean. She looks like I felt when I arrived in Vegas, disheveled, in need of a shower, and less shiny than I was when I started my journey.

The closer we get, the slower my steps become. The familiar beep of the key fob has me stilling about five feet from her.

"The license plate has been changed, registered to a different car, but we found your plates in the front trunk compartment. I also found your wallet under the passenger seat, driver's license still in it. But no money or credit cards." Det. Bryant opens the driver's door, looking back at me. "You want to…"

I step back, shaking my head, heart racing as the pine-scented air freshener washes over me. I can smell that night. The scent of him. Flashes of him bombard my vision. "No, no, no…" I turn away. I didn't want—

"Hey, hey. You're okay." Landry pulls me to a stop and into his arms. "No one is going to hurt you."

"It's not him," I whisper into his chest, burying my face and trying to recall all the mug shots of aimless faces. None of them is his. "He's still out there."

"We'll find him, Taylor," Det. Bryant says from behind me. "We have his fingerprints. He's just not in our system. But he'll screw up. He already did by losing your car."

Cap asks why it didn't go to a chop shop. I tune them out as the detective tells him what he already told me when I asked earlier, as I never expected to see my car again. With that thought, I glance around for Landry. I feel bad for not wanting my car anymore, but she's tainted by the memory of *him*. And I have no desire to be stricken with sense memories every time I'm near or ride in her.

The ride home is long and quiet. Cap is handling the details of getting my car back to Texas when it's released in the next few days. I don't go to work that night. Landry gave me the night off. I appreciate the consideration. Working probably would have been good for my mind. But being in a room full of people would do nothing for my nerves that are shot, wondering if Beau is just around the corner coming for me, reminding me what he took from me beyond the physical, beyond grief and a sense of self.

Instead, I spend my night playing with the twins and holding Iris, watching a movie with Cap and Cher, feeling more and more like a family I just might actually belong to after all.

But when it's time to sleep, it's hard-earned and restless, visions of Beau taunting me, taking from me, leaving my dignity on the side of a road where he left me.

CHAPTER 18

A WEEK LATER, AFTER JESS DROPS ME OFF AT HOME after our shifts at the bakery, and before it's time to get ready for my shift at Mel's, there's a knock at the door. Cap beats me to it, trying to catch them before they make too much racket with the kids and Cher napping.

"Delivery for Ms. Taylor Jamie Permian-O'Dair." The man on the front porch eyes me over Cap's shoulder.

"That's me."

He thrusts a small tablet in my hands. "Please sign on the line."

I glance at it and back to him. "What am I signing for?"

"Oh, sorry, I assumed you knew." He steps back, pointing to the driveway. "Your new car."

Holymotherfullofgracewhat?

"Barrett," Cap grumbles, taking the stairs two at a time.

I follow, stopping short to take in the pearly white SUV.

"It's a Maserati Levante Trofeo. It's a V8, 3.8-liter with a 580 horse-power engine," the delivery guy drones on.

He lost me at V8. It's pretty, though. "Who's it from?"

The man checks his tables. "Barrett O'Dair."

Cap was right and swivels, reading me. "Have you spoken to him?" No judgment in his tone.

"Only to tell him my car was coming to him, and he could do whatever he wants with it. I don't want it. He wasn't all that happy about it," I admit.

"Well, I guess this is his reply." Cap opens the driver's door. "It's a beauty."

"Yeah." I move a little closer, not hating the idea of having a new car that Cap or Cam didn't have to buy for me. But do I want to owe Barrett? And do I want another expensive car to make thieves notice me? Would a less expensive car make me invisible? "It's too much."

"It's not too much, Taylor. Take it. You need a car. Barrett can afford it. Let him splurge. Ease his guilt from lying to you all these years. It's a win-win."

I stare at Cap in surprise. I didn't think he'd want me to take anything from Barrett. They don't have the best relationship. He doesn't talk about him much. I just assumed he'd prefer I didn't have anything to do with Barrett, not that Cap is the reason I haven't been talking to the man I thought was my father.

I'm still mad at him and Mom for lying to us all these years.

We missed out on knowing our real dad. I missed out on hearing my mom talk about her time with Cap. He's told me a little, but out of respect for Cher, I don't ask about those times. I haven't even read the letter from my mom yet. I found out about Cap when I overheard a heated phone call between Barrett and Cam. Barrett should learn never to have sensitive conversations on speakerphone. Cam was pushing for Barrett to tell me Cap was my biological father. Barrett disagreed, obviously.

Cap approaches like he's not sure if I'll run or break down in tears. Both are highly likely nowadays. "You never have to ignore Barrett on my account, Taylor." He squeezes my hands. "He raised you, and though I'm sad I didn't get to be a part of it, I want you to have the type of relationship

97

you want with him, with me and Cher. Don't let our hang-ups skew your opinion of us or the relationships you want."

"I'm mad at him."

He nods. "You have every right to be." He motions to the car. "Him giving you a car is a replacement of the one stolen, a peace offering maybe. It doesn't obligate you to forgive him. Take it or don't. It's up to you." He kisses my cheek and motions to the delivery guy still waiting on me to sign.

I can always send it back.

I sign and accept the key fobs and paperwork, wishing the guy a good day as he hops in the dealership car that followed him here.

Cap pulls me into his side when he wraps an arm around my shoulder. "Now, the question is, are you going to let your old man drive this beauty?"

I drop one of the fobs in his hand. "It's all yours."

He stops me as I start to head inside. "On second thought, I think I'd rather try it out from the passenger seat. Why don't you take me for a quick spin?"

"I—"

"Just around the block. Maybe to Rowdy's and back." The softness in his gaze tells me I can say *no*, but he hopes I don't.

He's a sneaky guy, my bio dad, coaxing me into getting behind the wheel again.

It feels huge when I'm in the driver's seat. "I'm not used to sitting this high."

"Take a minute to familiarize yourself with the controls, get your seat situated and programmed, your mirrors set. I'm in no rush." He's such a liar. I know Cher is waiting on him to bring her food. But he's giving me this, and I truly appreciate it.

"Maybe we should pick up lunch." I arch a brow, not even bothering to hide my smile. There's no fear. It's been a while since I've even considered getting behind the wheel again, riding was hard enough. But today, with him, it feels right—it's time to find and reclaim my sea legs, so to speak.

He rubs his hands together and pats the dash. "Now you're talking. Whatever you're feeling, I'm there for it."

I'm laughing as I pull out of the driveway and onto the neighbor-hood street. Cap and Rowdy have the largest acreages of land that have houses on them. So it takes a few before I round the corner and see other houses. When we get to Cam's street, he's standing on the corner, waving like a fool. I glance at Cap before stopping next to my brother and pow-ering down the window. "What are you doing?"

"I heard we were making a food run. I'm hungry." He reaches for the back door seconds after it unlocks.

I flash to Cap, who only smiles. He's happy. My heart flutters, know-ing I have something to do with that.

As I drive us to pick up greasy hamburgers and fries, it dawns on me that Cam isn't normally home at this time of the day. He's usually still working out at the gym. "You set this up, didn't you?" I ask Cap.

"I have no idea what you're talking about." His eyes remain out the window. "I'm just enjoying a ride with my kiddos."

And just like that, I started driving again.

CHAPTER 19

MY FRUSTRATION OVER TAYLOR AND HAVING NO idea how to help her has grown exponentially since returning home from Flagstaff. She's been showing up to her shifts, serving customers like her life depends on it and pouring her soul into each and every lyric she sings on Wednesday and Friday nights. My band follows with requests to sing a duet with my Songbird. I've been ignoring those requests. I've been keeping my distance from Taylor, and singing with her would be the opposite of keeping her at arm's length for her and for my sanity.

She needs time to heal from whatever happened during her trip to Vegas. She's not offering details. I'm not pushing.

Smack. I shake my head and bring a grumpy Gabriel into focus.

"What the fuck?" he growls.

"What the hell?" I stretch my jaw and crack my neck. "Did you just hit me?"

"Get your head straight, or get the fuck off the mat before you get hurt."

Too late for that. Though, he obviously pulled the punch or I'd be laid out flat like a pancake.

"You need a minute?" Jonah asks from the sidelines.

I could use a few years. Maybe travel back in time eight or so. "Nah, I'm good." I shake it off and focus on sparring with the man. "Try to hit me again," I tease the beast, dodging and swaying, getting my cocky on.

"You've got a death wish," Jonah mumbles.

"Oh, yeah, he does." Gabriel's evil grin only grows. "You want me to take off the brakes? Give you my all?"

"Yeah, give it to me." I dart toward him then back. "Hit me hard enough to forget."

I still. *Fuck. I shouldn't have said that.*

Gabriel's arms drop to his sides. His head tilts, his anger morphing into concern. "Jonah, we're gonna need a minute." He tosses me a towel. "Come on." He snags our waters and walks out the back door, bare feet and all.

I follow like the good soldier I am. He's the king around here. Rowdy's second-in-command. He drops onto one of the benches Cap put out here a while ago, staring at the lake.

He waits.

I wait. Drinking my water. Taming my racing heart. Kicking myself for such a stupid, telling remark.

"You gotta tell her." His gruff statement throws me off.

I'm not ready to go there. "Tell who what?"

He side-eyes a glare that could skin a cat. "Don't waste my time."

"I want this fight."

"I know."

"I mean it."

"I'm not doubting you."

"Then why are we out here?" I point at the lake. It's beautiful, but I'm not going to win a fight admiring the view.

"Because you need to unload."

"I don't."

"Then you'll lose the fucking fight, let Cap down, let the guys down."

Fuck. Fuck. Fuck. "I can't—"

"You can. I'm here. Talk."

I can't. It's not my story to tell. But, God, it would be nice to get it off my chest, get another opinion.

He lets out a deep exhale and leans forward, his arms on his knees. "Look. You met me when I was in the worst spot of my life. You helped me get ready for my title fight regardless of how fucked I was over my Angel. Let me help you." He points to the gym. "Then we can get back to me helping you in the ring."

I nod but have no idea where to begin. I search the lake's edge as if it might have the answer.

When I take too long, he prompts, "When did you meet?"

"We were seventeen."

"You mean *you* were seventeen."

Frowning, I lock eyes with him. "No. *We* were seventeen."

He shakes his head. "Taylor is a year younger than Rowdy. You're a year *older* than him."

"The fuck!" I jump to my feet, stomping away, then turn, arms swinging wide. "She..." I can't even. "She was—"

"Fifteen," he fills in what I can't even comprehend. He stands. "She lied."

No. No. No. I cover my mouth with my hand, my fingers bruising my jaw. "Fuck!" It's muffled and not nearly as satisfying as I'd hoped, but stringing out a line of curses isn't going to make this revelation any easier to swallow.

"She said she was seventeen," I whisper as he nears. Emotions burn the back of my eyes as I plead with him to be wrong.

Rowdy's sister was only fifteen. I thought he was going to kill me before. I'm beyond dead now.

Gabriel grips my shoulder. "I helped her get her Nevada driver's license. I saw her birth certificate."

"She lied?" She lied to me. The gut-wrenching twist is back, like it was the day she no-showed, and each morning after, until I drowned her out with alcohol and partying with my friends. It was one long party that cost me my throwing arm and my football career.

"She lied." If she lied to me about her age, what else did she lie about? Did she even love me, or was I just a means to a great week to kick back with the poor dude on spring break? Did I lose my shit over a fling?

He nods. "I'm sorry. Didn't mean to make it worse."

"Nope." I shrug him off, heading toward the back door. "You reminded me I don't really know her. Never did." I want to throw up. I want to rage at her, at the world, but hitting Gabriel might work too. "You coming?" I throw over my shoulder.

His heavy sigh and weighted, "Right behind you," hits my ears before the door closes behind me.

With renewed vigor and anger, I drive into Gabriel with hit after hit. He takes it with a grunt and feeds it back to me. Each sting of contact only fuels my fury.

Gabriel once told me Cap taught him how to use his anger to fight and win. I guess I wasn't angry enough to understand it then, but now I feel like I might Hulk out if I don't fight. I guess I found the fuel I needed to win my fight.

Her fingers run up my arm, and I want to hurl. Instead, I let my eyes travel down her face to her perky tits she's all too happy to show me as she leans over the bar, her ass in the air, perched over the barstool to grab a cocktail napkin I forgot to give her. Delilah is a regular. She flirts like it's a sport. She's harmless, which is why I'm letting her hang on my every word like I'm speaking the gospel to a crowd of parishioners desperate for a healer.

Careful, sweetheart. There are no miracles or healing to be found here.

"You really should come. It's a blast." She slides her business card my direction with her cell number circled.

I pocket her card with no intention of calling, but my curious Songbird is watching, so… "I'll check my schedule and let you know."

Going to a Raiders' game is the last thing I want to do, even if it is in one of the luxury corporate suites she's gushing over. That could have been me on the NFL field. I've no desire to watch other, more talented athletes who didn't fuck up their chances over a girl who lied and ghosted them.

Fuck. Now I'm pissed all over again. I run my fingers through my hair, give Delilah a wink and ignore Taylor as she sidles up to the end of the bar to place an order. I move to the opposite end, directing Jake to take care of Taylor. I'm not ready to deal with her. I'm going with the *if you can't say anything nice, don't say anything at all* tactic.

On a run to the office, Ruby steps out of the ladies' room as I near. She pushes into me, tits pressed against my chest, bottom lip caught between her teeth as she lets a guy slide behind her to get to the men's room. "Fancy meeting you here." She bats her spider lashes, thinking she's seductive and tempting. Once again, all I want to do is hurl instead of let her flirt with me, much less touch me.

Out of the corner of my eye, I spot my blonde Heartbreaker as she comes out of the bathroom. My arched brow meets Ruby's smirk. She knew Taylor was right behind her. Sneaky wench. I grip Ruby's hips, none too gently, and turn us till my back is to Taylor, who stands there gawking. When I still don't hear footsteps, I say over my shoulder, "Don't you have work to do?"

She practically squeaks and stomps off. I can feel her hurt from here, but it only makes me madder. Who is she to get hurt when she's the liar in this relationship?

Ruby takes my actions as permission to run her hands over my chest, pressing up until her lips are even with mine. "It's about time, Cowboy."

Checking to confirm we're alone, I set Ruby back a few feet. "Never going to happen."

"But—"

"I needed a deterrent."

"And now?" she clucks, hands on her hips.

"Now I don't."

"You're a jerk. You know that?"

"Yep. Now get back to work."

"And if I don't?"

"Don't bother finishing your shift. You're replaceable. Don't forget who's the boss."

I walk away before I say something nastier that isn't truly meant for her at all. She's collateral damage, and I can't muster a fuck to give about it.

CHAPTER 20

SWIPE AT THE CORNER OF MY EYES. I DON'T THINK this day could get any worse. It started out good. I drove my new car for the first time to work. I was excited to share the news with Landry, only to find him locked in his office until the Mel's opened and then witness him work the bar and flirt with every human with boobs. But catching him with his hands on Ruby was the last straw.

I punch through the crowd, making my way to the stage, not even waiting for Leo to introduce me. I test the mic is live, pick up my guitar, slinging the strap over my head. and then strum my girl, testing her out before starting the intro to "Fingers Crossed."

I belt out the hate and lies he must have told me, having his fingers crossed when he said he loved me. By the time I hit the chorus for the second time, there's a group of women singing along with me, pouring their hearts into each callous word.

They get me. They *feel* me.

As I close the song, I catch Landry leaning on the wall near the hallway to his office, arms crossed, head low. He gives a soft nod before he disappears around the corner. I scan the bar and settle when I find Ruby serving drinks, laughing and winning hearts and those big tips she boasts about. But at least she's not with him.

Jealousy fuels the rest of my set, agitation growing to near mind-numbing proportions. When my time is up, I thank the crowd and practically knock over Ray, Landry's drummer, trying to get off the stage. He grips my arm. "Hey, you okay?"

"Not even a little." I tear away from him. I ignore everyone who tries to talk to me on my way to the employee lounge to put my guitar away.

My head down, I run smack dab into a chest and stumble back. "Shit. Sorry," I gasp.

Strong hands grip my arms, steadying me. "Settle, James," is whispered in my ear before releasing me so hard I spin.

That voice. "What?" I turn, scanning the room.

His words echo in my head. My heartbeat thrums in my ears. "Where are you?" I turn, only finding blank, confused faces staring back at me. Not his.

But he's here. I *heard* him.

"Where are you?!" The room closes in. Faces sway before my eyes. I gasp for air, dropping to my knees, losing my guitar in the fray of legs and feet.

The air is too thin.

When I fall forward, my hands sting with a smack to the hardwood floor. My stomach lurches. I dry heave. The buzz around me muffles in the mix of my body's protest against the flashing memories. *Settle, James.*

"Give her some fucking room!" bellows from in front of me as I'm swept into someone else's strong arms.

"Move!" The hard chest below my ear rattles as he carries me off, securing me tighter as I hide from the world inundating me with too much input. "You're okay, Taylor. I've got you."

Hearing *his* voice—the edge, the anger—brings my thoughts into focus. "No!" I struggle. "Put me down, Landry."

He can't touch me.

Not him.

Not him.

Not him.

"Hey, hey, Taytay." Jess' warm hand hits my back. "Let us help you." He kisses my temple when I peek out from Landry's chest.

"Jess." I practically lunge for him, my shock shattered enough I can move again.

"Fuck." He manages to catch me, but barely.

I wrap around him, not giving him a choice but to take me the rest of the way.

"What the fuck, Taylor?" Landry growls behind me, touching my hair, trying to see my face.

I arch away. "Don't touch me."

"Whoa. What?" Landry doesn't understand. I can't stand his touch. Not now. Not right after…

Settle, James.

"Taylor, it's Landry. He'd never hurt you," Jess insists, but he has no idea. Landry already has.

He can be cold one minute and warm the next. "No." I extricate myself from Jess and stumble away, finding I'm in Landry's office. It's only the three of us. I take a few cleansing breaths, swiping at my face, knowing it's a lost cause. "I need to go."

"No. Wait. What happened?" Landry steps forward to touch me.

I step back till I hit the filing cabinet on the far wall. He's a toucher, but I can't have the memories in my head and his hands on me. Not like this. Not when I'm upset and mad at him. Not when all I want is his comfort and all I've gotten today is the cold shoulder. Not when there's another man in my head, confusing me, making my skin crawl. I have to get out of here. I can't think when he has my broken heart swimming in the same pool as Beau. They're not the same. They are *not* the same! "I wasn't asking for permission."

He slides his hands in his front pockets. "What happened? Someone scared you. Touched you?" He reaches for me then pulls back. "You just had a fucking panic attack. You can't drive home, not in this state."

I laugh, which morphs into a sob. God, I'm losing it in front of them. "Just watch me."

"Taylor," he tries again, offering his hand. "Please."

I lock on Jess. "I need my purse and guitar."

"On it." He opens the door and stops short. Leo is standing there, looking like he'd rather be anywhere else.

"Right here." Leo holds my purse and case up. "I thought you might want them."

"Thanks." I grab my things and rush out the back door before they can stop me.

"Taylor!" all three guys call.

I don't stop.

At my car, I open the back door, tossing in my case with less care than she deserves. I still when I spot the piece of paper stuck to the driver's side window. It's wedged between the glass and the trim. I snatch it up, thinking it's a ticket. Why would I get a ticket in a parking lot? I'm not parked illegally. It's a new car. It has all its plates, registration and inspection sticker.

I turn it over. My skin pricks as the blood drains from my face and my stomach drops.

No. Please, no.

"What does it say?"

I shove the paper in my purse. "None of your business." I climb in, close and lock my doors before Landry even considers I'd run from him.

He should have considered it. He should be happy. He's done nothing but push me away—with blinding moments of pulling me closer.

I start the car, putting it in drive.

"Taylor!" He bangs on my window. "Don't drive like this. Let me take you." With crazy eyes, he points behind him. "Let Jess take you. Please," he pleads.

"I'm fine." I edge forward. When I'm sure I won't hit him or the others, I floor it out of the parking lot.

I grab my phone and quickly find the number I'm looking for.

"Taylor?" Detective Bryant answers on the first ring, his voice filling my car from its speakers.

I glance at the clock, concerned it's too late to be calling and thrown by his greeting. "How did you know it was me?"

"You're in my contacts. What's wrong?"

"He's here. He found me." My admission releases more tears.

"Where's *here*?" The alert in his voice settles me. I was afraid he wouldn't take my call. Take me seriously. I'm not even in his state any longer.

"Vegas. Mel's Bar, where I work."

"You saw him? When?"

"Just now. Like five minutes ago. But…"

"But what?"

"I didn't actually *see* him. It was crowded. He grabbed me and whispered *Settle, James* in my ear. Then I found a note on my car window. It's the first time I've driven my new car to work. I just got it. How did he know which car was mine?"

"James? That's the nickname he called you because you were named after James Taylor, right?"

And Cap. "Yeah." I can't believe I shared that detail with Beau. What other stupidly personal stuff did I share in the hours we were on the road that I don't remember?

"What did the note say?"

"I'm… I can't remember it word for word. I'm driving. I'm almost home. I can send you a picture."

"Yes, text it to me. I'm also going to call the local PD and have them come collect it and dust your car for prints."

"Okay," my voice breaks.

"You're okay otherwise, though? He didn't hurt you again?"

"No." Who knows what he'd have done if we'd been alone.

"Good. That's good." He sounds nearly as relieved as I am. "I'll stay on the phone until you get home, but I need to put you on mute just for a minute while I call this in. But I'm here. I can hear you if you need me. Okay?" He's being so nice.

"Okay. And thank you. I'm sorry to call you so late."

"No apology necessary. I'm glad you did. I'll be right back, but remember, I can hear you. Just holler if you need me."

"Okay."

The line is silent as I drive the rest of the way home, except for my sniffles and sighs to calm my heart, not another word is spoken till I pull into the driveway. "Oh, God," I cry. *He's here!*

"What?! What is it?!" Det. Bryant comes on the line.

"It's… It's—" The dark figure moves into the light. Holy. "It's Cap," I cry harder. "He standing out front waiting for me."

"I'm glad he's there. Can you let me talk to him? Don't turn your car off in case it disconnects."

I try to breathe through my relief and quiet my fears. "Yeah." I put the car in park and unlock the doors seconds before Cap opens mine.

"Tay." He pulls me into his arms, unbuckling my seat belt.

But before he can pull me out, I let him know, "Detective Bryant is on the phone."

Caps' brows rise. "Detective?"

"Hi, James. Do you think you can take me off the car speaker?"

I grab my purse and hand him my phone. "I'll head inside."

Cap grips my hand. "You sure? I can call him back."

"No. It's okay—" Headlights blind me. "What the…"

A truck comes to a screeching halt behind my car.

"It's Landry." Cap closes himself inside my car, believing I'm safe with him.

I'm not so sure. He looks really mad as he stalks toward me.

"Don't ever fucking do that again," Landry seethes, stopping inches from me, getting in my face, knocking me off-balance.

Why is he so upset? I'm the one who was scared. I'm the one hurt by his actions tonight before the incident with Beau.

"You scared the shit out of me tonight when you went down to the floor. Then you wouldn't let any of us help you." He tugs at his hair, his eyes a little wild and a lot hurt. "*Then* you drive like a bat out of hell, tears streaming down your face. You could have had a wreck. You could have—"

He's worried. I place my hand over his pounding heart. "I'm okay."

He sucks in air. His hands are on his hips, head down, fighting for control. "It's not okay, baby. You can't lock me out like that."

"Really?" I drop my hand and step back. "You want to talk about locking out? You've given me nothing but the cold shoulder since I've arrived in Vegas and worse since Flagstaff. You run hot and cold crueler than any Texas weather that can't decide what fucking temperature it wants to be." I poke at his chest. "Then you let women drape themselves all over you, practically showing you their breasts, flirting with you while you tell me to *get back to work.*" I mimic him by lowering my voice and barking the last four words.

Cap rolls down the window. "Everything okay out here?" His eyes flash between Landry and me.

"We're good." Landry sighs, stepping back.

Cap waits for my confirmation.

"I'm good." I won't say *we're* good because there is no *we* in this equation.

Cap rolls the window up and resumes his conversation with the detective. I can't make out what they're saying, but I hear their muffled voices.

Before I can say another word, a police car with flashing lights pulls in behind Landry. Cap must disconnect the call because, a moment later, my car is off, and Cap emerges with my phone, handing it to me. When I start to slide it into my purse, he stops me. "Detective Bryant is still on the line. He wants to speak to you."

Oh. I step back, bringing it to my ear. "Hey."

"Hey. You better?"

"Yeah. Now that I'm home. Thanks for hanging with me."

"Sure. Listen, the police who arrived are the ones on duty. They'll take your statement and the note. Don't forget to send me a picture first. Then they'll dust your car for prints. It shouldn't take long. I'll talk to the local crimes unit in the morning and fill them in on the rest. You don't need to rehash the whole thing with them. Cap has your case number.

They can refer to that in their report. You only need to tell them about tonight. Okay?"

"And if they ask for more details?"

"You let Cap handle them. He'll tell them to refer to the case or to me."

"Thanks again, Detective Bryant."

"You're welcome, Taylor. I'll be in touch tomorrow after I talk to the Vegas detective assigned to your case."

"Okay."

"Oh, and Taylor, don't go anywhere by yourself. Understand?"

Shit. My nerves spike again. *He's here.* "Yeah, okay."

After we disconnect and before I deal with the new cops, I turn my back, take the note from my purse and take a picture, texting it to Det. Bryant's cell.

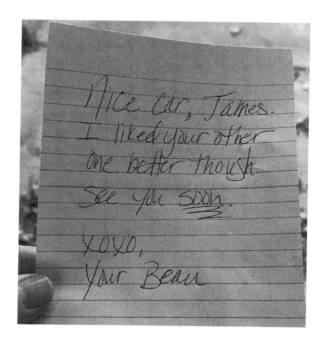

I want to throw up.

CHAPTER 21

CHER HAS TAYLOR TUCKED INTO HER SIDE ON THE couch as Cap finishes up with the police officers who showed up to take her statement and the note the asshole left her, and dust her car for prints. Feeling useless in my skin that feels too tight, I stand sentry, wanting to be the one to comfort my Songbird *and* be the one who takes care of the cops. Currently, I'm neither. I'm just the discarded ex, temperamental boss, and wannabe friend who doesn't know which way is up when it comes to her.

I was an ass earlier. I was pissed and acting like an idiot to push her away, too wrapped up in my own shit to remember she has something bigger and far more important going on than my hurt feelings.

I was coming out to apologize, wanting to catch her after her set, before she went back to serving. I didn't make it in time to see what happened. I'd only rounded the corner from the office, coming up short when I witnessed her disappear in the crowd, dropping out of sight. My heart dropped with her.

It took me a second to comprehend what was happening. Panic and anger fought for dominance as I pushed through the crowd to find her on all fours in a blind panic, heaving like her insides had done her wrong.

My instinct to save, comfort, extricate her from the situation overran the logic that perhaps being manhandled was not what she needed. Yet she let Jess touch her. She practically leapt from my arms into his.

It was *my* touch she didn't want. That knowledge burns my regret into my soul. She didn't want my help.

Does she still feel that way?

Have I pushed too far?

Are my mistakes too great to come back from?

Are hers?

Is it fair to still be butthurt about her leaving me when we were kids? She didn't have a choice. She was young, couldn't even drive yet. What was she supposed to do? Run away? To where? Would she have known how to find me in Dallas? Did I give her enough details? She had my full name and my phone number. She knew where I played football. Her parents didn't keep her phone forever. She could have reached out to me at least once in the months that followed, but instead she left me high and dry, wrecked with silence, and my own imagination of the reasons she never contacted me too dark to explore.

I want to pretend we've already worked through it all, forgiven each other, and move forward, forgetting she broke my heart and my ability to love and trust another woman.

I want to hold her when she's sad.

I want to love her when she's cantankerous and believing she's unworthy.

I want to live in her sunshine when she unleashes her life-altering smile because of something I did or said.

I want to be the reason she stays.

The reason she never leaves.

The reason for each and every day that follows.

I want to be her reason.

I want to be the person who helps her find her inner glow that's been missing.

I want to be her rock, be whatever is it she needs.

I need her to forgive me for my actions since she arrived in Vegas.

When the cops finally leave, Cap ambles over, pulling his oldest daughter into his arms. I have to look away. It hurts knowing he's hers because he's my boss, my family by choice. Yet, I'm more than tempted to fuck that all up for her if it means we get a second chance.

"You doing okay?" he asks.

"Yeah." She pulls away first, looking anywhere but at the three of us. "I'm sorry I brought this to your door." She glances at me but won't hold my gaze. "And your bar."

"No—" I start to rebuff her but get cut off by the little dynamo.

"What?!" Cher stands in front of Taylor. "You didn't do this. He brought himself here. You can't control his actions. You did the right thing calling the detective, bringing the Vegas PD into this."

Cap pulls Cher into his side, kissing her temple. But his words are for Taylor. "You can't go anywhere alone. Not until this guy is caught. He's feeling brave. Showing up at your place of work, taunting you. He'll try again." He looks to me before focusing back on his daughter. "I know you don't want to talk about it, but we need to know the extent of his crimes. We need understand how far he's gone. How far he's willing to go."

Cher buries her head in Cap's chest. She went through a lot with Gabriel and Reese's father. This has to be hitting too close to home—bringing up old stuff.

He whispers something in her ear, only for her. She shakes her head in response and tightens her grip before reaching a hand out to Taylor, who takes it without hesitation.

"Did he hurt you, Taylor?" Cap's voice is gruff, coated with emotions and the strain to stay in control.

When Taylor starts shaking, with tears falling in rapid fire, I can't take it anymore. I pull her into my arms, kissing her head and whispering, "It's okay, Songbird. We got you."

We don't need her words. It's obvious that asshole did more than just steal her car and belongings. He took something far more valuable.

I latch on to Landry with no intention of letting go. His strength comforts me and is exactly what I need despite our past—or maybe because of it. He's the only one who can give me this.

"It's late. Let's get some sleep and talk more in the morning." Cap sweeps his thumb across my cheek, then kisses the same spot. "You need us, no matter the time or place, we're here for you."

Cap cuts his gaze to Landry, who's quick to reply, "I'm not leaving." His hold on me is firm and determined. I don't mind it at all.

Cap pats him on the back with a knowing smile. "I figured as much."

Cher gives me a silent hug as Cap locks up the house and arms the security alarm, coming back to take her hand. "See y'all in the morning."

The silence after they're gone feels deafening.

Landry rubs my back, his cheek lying on my head, swaying gently. "You need anything before bed—food, water?"

I pull back using the sleeves of my t-shirt to dry my face. "Yeah, some water. Maybe food." His surprise has me chuckling. "I'm one of those girls who eats when upset." I shrug and turn for the kitchen. He did offer.

"I could eat." His hand lands on my lower back as he follows, reminding me of all the things I've missed about him: his tender ways, his possessiveness, his ability to see through my blustering and find the heart of me. Or at least he used to. I don't know anymore. He may not even care to look.

He opens the fridge, eyeing its contents. "What do you feel like?"

"Maybe just a sandwich." I slip under his arm to stand in front of him. "I think there's some chicken salad." I glance up at him. "Or we have turkey and ham if you'd prefer that."

He grabs the mayo out of the door. "I'm easy. I'll have whatever you're having."

"Chicken salad sandwiches it is."

Tummy full and a quick shower later, I enter my bedroom to find Landry standing there staring at a pair of pajama bottoms in his hand. "Where'd those come from?"

His head pops up, his furrowed brow aimed at me. "Cap."

I start laughing. "That must have been awkward."

"Tell me about it." He lifts his hand. "He just came in and handed them to me. Didn't say a word." He runs his fingers through his hair. "I don't know if it's a warning to keep my damn dick covered or a sweet gesture to be sure I had something comfortable to sleep in."

I pat his tummy as I walk by. Damn, I forgot how toned he is. "I bet it's both. Shower's all yours if you want it. Oh." I dig in my underwear drawer and pull out a pair of black boxer briefs. "They're yours."

He quirks a brow and eyes the briefs in my hand before locking on me.

"You left them in my room in Padre."

"You kept them all these years?"

"I never had the heart to throw them out." That admission hurts more than I anticipated.

I turn toward the bed before he can see my blush. "And no, no one has worn them besides you." And me, but I'm not about to admit that.

"Taylor."

The rumble in his voice sends chills along my spine, which I ignore as I slip under the sheets. "Turn off the light on your way to the bathroom, would ya?"

I've held it together long enough. If I have to admit how much I've cherished that stupid pair of briefs, I've no doubt I'll crumble. And I don't think even he can put me back together.

CHAPTER 22

SILENTLY SLIDE INTO BED BESIDE HER IN ONLY MY boxer briefs that smell freshly laundered. I was disappointed they didn't smell like her. Didn't stop me from beating off in the shower to visions of her wearing them all these years, thinking of me when she did.

It says something she took them with her from Padre Island. Says even more that she kept them all this time. I've no doubt I would have done the same if she'd gifted me with one of her sexy-as-fuck thongs she wore back then. Though, honestly, I probably would have burned them in a drunken rage. I was too hurt to be sentimental.

She snuggles into me when I wrap an arm around her waist, pulling her into my chest. She may not need the contact, but I do. I shouldn't have been able to get hard knowing—or thinking I know—what that bastard did to her. But the sight of her blush before she turned away after giving me my underwear was enough to incite a riot in my pants. I knew if I didn't take care of it, I'd be hard all night, and I sure as shit don't want to scare her or traumatize her by being inappropriately sexual after what she's been through.

On a sigh, she reaches over, pulling my arm below her head. I take over when I realize what she wants: her snug against my chest and my arms fully wrapped around her—one around her chest the other around her middle and my bent legs spooning hers. Muscle memory has me kissing her neck before I can stop myself.

"Shit. I'm sorry. I—"

"It's fine." She squeezes my arms with hers. "I've never minded your kisses, Dually. I never will."

She hasn't called me that in eight years. It feels like too much, jumping intimacy boundaries we haven't earned. Yet here I am wrapped around her like we used to, like no time has passed.

"I think he drugged me," she whispers into the dark.

I flinch but try to cover it by pulling her tighter against me. "You don't have to," I assure her. "But I'm here."

"I'll tell you, then you tell Cap and Cam. I can't. Detective Bryant knows. But I can't tell—"

"I got you. Whatever you need, I'll do it."

She's quiet for so long, my heart beating against her back, I think she's changed her mind, until she continues, "I felt safe with him. I mean, I didn't even think about *safe*. It just felt natural, like he was a bud. I don't even know how it happened, really. How I could be so stupid, think I was so untouchable to let a stranger in my car. He sat at my table at a diner in New Mexico, and the next thing I know, he's in my car driving with me to Vegas. He was nice and easygoing. Not a threatening bone in his body— but again, I wasn't even thinking in those terms of safe or not. There was no spark, no sexual tension. It was like one of my brother's friends tagging along for the ride. Bland and okay."

Was he really that nice or conning her from the start? I'm betting on the latter.

"Hours later, we stopped for food, but instead of eating in the car, he suggested we stop at a rest stop, eat at a picnic table. There, in that moment, I second-guessed if it was a smart thing to be doing—eating at night at a too-quiet rest stop. I wasn't considering *he* was the danger. I was worried about the location; anyone could come out of the dark and attack us. I was worried about *us*, not me."

I grip her hip, wanting to see her face, gauge what she needs me to do beyond holding her. But she keeps going. I don't want to stop her even though every second listening to her berate herself for not being more fearful is killing me, eating at my insides.

"It gets fuzzy from there. I went to the restroom. Came out feeling a little drunk, but I hadn't had anything to drink except the soda he bought me at the vending machine at the rest stop when I finished my bottled water with dinner. Thought maybe motion sickness, food poisoning... He was waiting, steadied me, helped me to the car. I told him I felt weird. He acted like everything was fine. And still, no alarm bells went off.

"The next thing I know, I'm in my car, but all I see are the tall trees out the windows and the roof of my car. I didn't get 'the sideways' then, but now I understand my seat was laid back and my back and head were on the middle console. I don't know." She shakes her head. "It's fuzzy, like I was coming in and out of consciousness. I couldn't focus. Then—" her voice cracks.

I hold her tighter, whispering, "It's okay." I'm going to kill the guy, but she's okay. In this moment, I have her.

"One minute I'm staring at trees and the dark sky, and the next we're... He's..."

I try to quell my rising anger, but it's of little use. I'm going to rip the guy's dick out through his throat when they find him.

"I was fading in and out. I think. But at one point I must have started fighting him because I remember him holding me down hard, saying, *Settle, James.*"

Her voice cracking again as she sobs is all I can take. I sit up and pull her into my lap, burying my head in her neck. "I'm so fucking sorry, Taylor." Her hold on me, on my heart is monumental. "So, so, so sorry."

"Tonight, when he grabbed me, he whispered, *Settle, James.* That's how I knew it was him without even seeing his face. He wanted me to know. I can't get his voice out of my head."

"I wish I could take the memories away, baby. I truly do."

She nods. "Me too."

"What happened next? How did you make it to Vegas?" I want her to get it all out instead of bearing it alone.

"At one point, he moved us to the grass for more room, I guess. I had an old blanket in the trunk to keep my guitar from banging around. I still couldn't move, couldn't control my movements. It's like I was there but wasn't. Then he was on me again. His words in my ear, telling me how good I was taking it. Like we were lovers, like I wanted him. But I didn't, Landry. I didn't," she cries. "I hated that I couldn't move to fight or run."

I capture her face, locking eyes, ensuring she hears me. "I know, Taylor. I'm so sorry that happened to you. You didn't do anything wrong." The pain on her face is devastating. "You didn't do anything to deserve that."

"I let him in my car? Who does that?"

"You trusted the wrong person. But that's never an excuse for what he did."

She lays her head on my chest under my chin. "I woke up the next morning sick as a dog, still lying on that damn blanket, naked, wishing it had been a bad dream, only my nightmare hadn't ended yet. He'd left my guitar case and my small duffel bag with a twenty tucked in the pocket sitting beside me. No purse, no ID, no phone. And, of course, neither he nor my car were anywhere in sight.

"A nice lady and her family helped me. They had an RV, fed me lunch and got me as far as the next town. They weren't heading to Nevada but gave me a hundred dollars. I ended up using too much of it on a motel and food, self-preservation mode. Slept for two days before I felt human again. The memories of what happened came back slowly, but nothing like they did tonight when I heard his voice."

"Why didn't you call your dad or Rowdy? You know they would have been there in a heartbeat." I would have dropped everything to rescue my Songbird.

She shrugs and slips off me, reaching for the Kleenex on the nightstand. After blowing her nose and drinking some water, with her back to me, she says, "I was in shock, I think. It didn't even dawn on me for a few days that I should have gone to the police right away. It took me a while to report it. I was too ashamed to call and ask for help. In the end, I only reported the car as stolen. I didn't report the rape until Detective Bryant pushed for more."

"I'm glad you did."

She lets out a soft sigh. "I doubt anything will come of it."

"They'll catch him, Taylor. I don't want you to worry about him. I'll keep you safe—we'll all keep you safe."

Her laugh is bitter. "Most days you can barely stand to look at me, Landry. I'm not even sure you like me anymore. I don't expect you to do anything for me." She shrugs again, and I'm really tired of the ambivalence in it. She's lost her fight, and it kills me. "I appreciate you being here and listening, but I don't expect anything. I know we can't go back. It's too late for us."

Is she for real right now?

"Taylor." I reach out, taking her hand and squeeze. "Do me a favor. Don't think for me or decide you know what's going on in my head unless I communicate it. I'm here because I'm worried and because I care. I've been as ass, and I'm sorry. When it comes to you, my hurt is deep and twisted with misunderstandings, untruths, and stupid choices on my end as a result."

"I hurt you, intentional or not," she whispers.

"And I hurt you right back. I'm so sorry."

She nods. I take that as her acceptance of my apology.

"And as for not being able to stand looking at you? It's because it hurts. I'm not supposed to know you in this life. Our... unclear history aside, you return out of nowhere like a right hook, *again*, knocking me completely sideways *again*. You're so fucking beautiful. I physically ache that I can't touch you, that you aren't *mine* to touch whenever I want, whenever *you* want."

Her sweet smile flashes over her shoulder and zaps straight to my heart. "Really? You still...?"

"Yeah, really." I pat the bed, lying down. "Now come back to bed. You need to sleep. You've had a shit-ass day. Let me hold you so we both know you're safe."

"Okay."

She climbs back in bed, under the covers, her head on my chest and half of her body wrapped around me.

It's pure torture.

It's pure heaven.

CHAPTER 23

"**T**AYLOR!" CAP'S VOICE PULLS ME FROM SLEEP seconds before my bedroom door flies open and my brother stomps into the room.

"What the fuck?" He glares at Landry, who's blinking awake, gripping me tighter under the covers.

"Rowdy, come downstairs. Let them wake up," Cap interjects, giving me a *sorry, I tried to warn you* look.

Cam's death stare doesn't waver.

"Hey, man. Give us a minute." Landry sits up, blocking me. "We'll be down in a few."

"You should have fucking called me last night," he rails at Landry, "and what? Now you're sleeping with my sister?" He turns his glare on Cap. "And *you* let him."

Landry is up in a flash, hand on Cam's chest. "You're upset. But let's remember who was really hurt in all of this and take it down a notch."

Cam scans Landry's bare chest and pajama bottoms. *Pajama bottoms? When did that happen?* Then he eyes me over Landry's shoulder. "You should have called me. *I'm* your fucking family."

Ouch, that hit like a punch to the gut. "I'm sorry. I thought Cap was *my* family too." I stand, not caring that I'm only in a sleepshirt and panties. "And who I *sleep* with is none of your business."

Landry pivots, crowding me back. "Hey, let's not make it worse. He's upset. He loves you. He's worried."

Damn, he's right. My head hits Landry's chest. He wraps me in his arms. "We'll be down in a minute," he says over his shoulder.

"Take your time," Cap says before the door shuts.

"I'm sorry about that." My hands press into his chiseled abdomen, wishing I could do more, trying to remember why I can't kiss him.

He cups my cheek, tipping my head back. "Why are you apologizing for your brother?"

I lock on his warm hazel eyes, rumpled hair, and a hint of a smile. "I don't like him yelling at you."

Landry shrugs and kisses my forehead. "He has a right to feel what he feels. I can take him yelling at me. But I won't stand for him yelling at you."

I hug him, taking a second to enjoy his warmth and the fact that he's allowing me to. "Where were you, growing up? I could have used someone on my side against my two older brothers. They were a huge pain in the ass."

"They still are."

"True."

He pats my butt. "Go. Do what you need to in the bathroom, so we can get down there before he comes looking for us."

"Okay." I'm halfway to the door before I turn back. "When did you put on the pajama bottoms?"

He smirks. "Earlier when I heard Iris crying. I figured everyone would feel better if I wasn't in my underwear."

"Humph." I open the door and wink over my shoulder. "I think having you out of them would make *me* feel better."

Bathroom used, teeth brushed, and a little more dressed—me in Cap's borrowed pajama bottoms and one of Rowdy's old shirts, and Taylor in purple sleep pants and the same shirt she slept in—we make our way downstairs to find everyone in the kitchen.

"Good morning." Cher pulls Taylor into a hug, a knowing smile on her face.

"Morning, Cher. It smells good in here."

"There's lots of food. Go sit. Eat," she coaxes her stepdaughter.

Cher surprises me with a hug. "You're a gift, Landry," she whispers, pulling back to pat my cheek, her eyes glassy like she might cry.

If she keeps being all sweet like this, I just might join her. I'm not really sure how to respond, but I know she wouldn't take it well if I accounted all the ways I'm absolutely *not* a gift. Today's not the day for me to unpack my baggage at her feet. So, I simply say, "Thanks," and kiss her on the cheek.

Taylor graces me with a smile as she takes my hand, pulling me to sit beside her at the kitchen table. Cher follows, taking the seat next to Cap, who gives both of us another apologetic look.

Before Rowdy can open his mouth, my Songbird shows her fortitude. "I know you have questions. But let's have a nice breakfast. There's time for yucky conversations to be had afterwards. Okay?" She looks to everyone before piling food on her plate.

Rowdy's stunned expression is priceless. He only nods and gets back to eating. Cap places a coffee carafe on the table, and I fill Taylor's cup and then mine. Taylor swaps her full plate for my empty one. I thought she was getting food for herself. I guess not. She only smiles and repeats the process of filling her plate.

We eat with light conversation, Cade and Wade serving as comic relief in their highchairs next to Cher and Cap. Baby Iris is taking her morning nap but should be up soon, according to Cher, which means Cap is nearly force-feeding Cher to be sure she eats before her ravenous daughter wakes up. I can't hide my smile, one Cher doesn't miss. She simply bows her head and returns to eating with a smile of her own.

I didn't have this family camaraderie I've found in Gabriel's, Rowdy's, and Cap's homes. It's always a mix of the same people, but the feeling of fellowship and home is the same no matter where we are. Being here reminds me I'm lucky to be considered part of their inner circle. I only hope my relationship—or more, my history—with Taylor doesn't jeopardize that for either of us.

After breakfast, Taylor kisses my cheek, motioning to her dad and brother. "Tell them what they need to know. I'm going to watch the boys while Cher takes a leisurely shower before Itty Bitty wakes up."

I stand and follow, making sure she's gone before I turn to the watchful eyes of her male family members. Stalling before I can find the right words, I refill my coffee and text Leo about not coming in today. His reply is quick and reduces my stress over not working tonight. I'm right where I need to be. I'd close down Mel's before leaving. I'm thankful I have Leo and don't need to.

After a coffee refill, I sit, facing Rowdy and Cap, hating that I have to tell them what they need to know. "Taylor gave me permission to share that Beau not only robbed her but also drugged and raped her."

"Fuck!" Rowdy's hand slaps on the table, rattling the dishes.

Cap's hands fly over his face as his shoulders start to shake. He's the only grown man I've seen cry, but last time it was when he married Cher. This is so very different.

"I prayed my suspicions weren't true," he moans.

"She doesn't remember a lot of it, but when he grabbed her last night and said something, it triggered her memories. They flooded in, and she had a panic attack," I share the last of the nasty news.

"I'd hoped she'd been spared." Rowdy rubs his eyes.

"Me too." I look away before I start to cry too.

"This is some serious shit." Cap pulls out his phone. "He's not just here to steal her new car. He wants *more* from her."

"He's not getting a repeat." Rowdy shakes his head in disgust and outrage.

"He's toying with her. He could have waited outside for her, taken her, but instead, he came inside to mess with her head. Let her know he can get to her wherever she is. He's been following her. Otherwise, how would he know what she drives and where she works?" I think on it some more. "He probably followed us from Flagstaff. Maybe letting that guy take her car from him was just a ploy to find her again, figuring she'd come to claim it."

"He's feeling cocky and brave. We can use that against him." Cap starts talking on the phone, facing away.

Rowdy leans in. "He's calling his DA friend. Cap has all kinds of contacts. He's going to arrange security at the bakery, gym, and Mel's."

"Fuck that. I can close Mel's."

"No," Cap interjects, turning back to the table. "It's the perfect place to catch him. It's crowded, and he's confident. He'll feel like he can slip in there undetected like he did before. The difference is, we'll be waiting next time."

A plan starts to form. Security's set to start immediately. I'll have a few new employees, and my Songbird will have her own personal bodyguard—me for one, but also an actual bodyguard for when one of us can't be with her.

CHAPTER 24

CAM LOCKS ME IN A BONE-CRUSHING HUG BEFORE he leaves. Cap is right behind him with nearly the exact hug, except he's not leaving. He's spending the day at home with his family, which he ensures includes me. "What Rowdy said earlier about *him* being your family—he is, of course, but so are we. *You* are my daughter, and even if you weren't, your heart and the fact that you're his sister would have made you family anyway. You. Are. My. Family." He kisses my forehead, whispering, "He was just upset. Felt left out." He releases me and goes in search of his wife and three littles.

Landry pulls me into his side when he spots my watery eyes. "Take it to heart because he means it. Family is important to Cap. *You* are important to him."

I'm amazed how the last twenty-four hours have changed things between Landry and me. His hostility and coolness have vanished. I feel more settled in my place in Cap and Cher's lives. And I can't believe Cap was fine with Landry sleeping with me. He doesn't know that nothing happened. And it doesn't mean I don't want something to happen. A pair of pajama bottoms wouldn't stop us anyway. I just didn't expect Cap to be so cool about it all.

I'm not a kid, though my choices of late are questionable. It's nice to be treated like an adult instead of a disappointing daughter like Barrett makes me feel, or an irritating sister like Drake and sometimes Cam make me feel.

"And what about you?" I dare ask.

"Well, I don't play hooky from work for just anyone." He motions to the couch. "Find us a movie. I'm going to grab some drinks."

When he comes back, he settles next to me, pulling me into his arms, my head on his chest, laying kisses on my brow as we start the movie. Barely five minutes in, I begin to drift off but jerk awake, fighting it. I give in a few moments later when he whispers softly, "Sleep, baby. I got you."

And he does. Sleeping with him in my bed or in his arms on the couch with my family coming in and out is heaven. It's a place I never thought I'd get to experience with him again. Rarely even considered trying with anyone else. Deep down, maybe I always knew it was him. I was just biding my time, growing up, becoming someone I hope he can love again… someday.

Sometime after lunch, he and Cher disappear into the kitchen, coming back with a huge bowl of popcorn. The twins go crazy as we watch a more kid-friendly movie with them camped out on the floor on blankets and pillows. For a split second I think about joining them but remember how much I cherish the man I'm using as a pillow.

And that's how the rest of the day goes.

None of us go to work. We cuddle on the couch watching movies alone or with Cap, Cher, and the kids. We eat delicious food that either Cher cooks or has ready in the fridge. When I'm tired, I nap. There are no awkward moments or hesitation to lean on Landry, cuddle under his arm, or lay my head in his lap.

It's heaven.

I don't think about Beau.

Or work.

Or family in Texas.

It's a wonderful cocoon of safety and acceptance with my new family and the man who has always held my heart despite how it ended and the devastating waves that continued to bombard my life long after.

Sitting on the edge of her bed, I'm studying a text from Cap about Taylor's bodyguard being here at seven AM. I'm not sure why he's texting me instead of Taylor. Not that I don't want to be in the know, it just puts me in the position of having to bring up the bad that's shadowing her life at the moment. We've finally had a great day of light and good. I hate to burst that bubble.

When Taylor walks in a moment later, I about swallow my tongue. She's in an oversized muscle shirt that hangs low under her arms, showing enough side tit to make a dead man hard. I don't even know if she's wearing panties, but by the look on her face and the fact she just locked the door, it's questionable.

I sit up straight and toss my phone to the nightstand as she sashays my direction. Damn, my Heartbreaker is all grown up, not that I hadn't noticed before, but this is a whole other level of sexy in barely any clothes, her tits jiggling with every step and hips taunting me to hold on to them as I shove every hard inch of me inside her on endless repeat.

Fuck. Me. I'm so screwed.

She stops mere inches away, her tits right below my nose at mouth level, nipples hard and begging for attention. Does she even know what she's doing? Is she teasing me on purpose?

The blush rising up her cheeks doesn't confirm anything other than she's noticed she has my full attention.

"What's on your mind, Songbird?"

She runs her fingers through my hair, edging closer, so fucking close I could bite a nip if my eyes weren't locked on hers.

Focus, dumbass. She's been hurt.

I swallow around the desire licking at my dominant side, urging me to roar her name, commanding she get naked and on all fours for the feasting.

I'm not the same guy I was when I was seventeen. She liked being under me, pleasing me, nearly as much as I needed to please her. But time and a locked-down heart have given free rein to my rougher tendencies that I rarely let show.

I grip her chin, ignoring her gasps, bringing her ever closer. "What are you doing, Taylor? You need something from me?"

She nods and bites her lip, shy and seductive, but a flash of fear flits across her face.

It's too soon.

I release her and lean back. "Get in bed. You need sleep. Your new bodyguard will be here bright and early to accompany you to the bakery."

She frowns. "How do you know this?"

"Cap texted me. I guess he thought I should tell you." His way of being a cock blocker.

She looks away seconds before rounding the bed and silently slipping under the covers. My back to her, I sit for as long as I can stand, trying to figure out if the hurt I saw on her face is because of me or Cap. When I hear sniffles, I lose the battle to stay over here.

I'm an asshole.

"Hey." I roll over, coming up on all fours, hovering over her. She's on her side, eyes downcast with tears rolling across her nose and landing on the bed. "I'm sorry. Please don't cry." *Or at least tell me you're not crying because of me.*

The tears don't stop. She won't even look at me. "I fucked up. I'm sorry. Tell me what I can do to make it right."

She flops to her back, red-rimmed eyes searching for lies or truth in mine. "I'm afraid to ask."

"Why?"

"Because I don't want you to say *no*."

My mind swirls with possible scenarios she'd ask of me that I'd say no to. "I'll do anything for you, Songbird. Just ask."

"Touch me." Her lips move, but I barely hear the impossible words she's asking.

I ignore my wayward thoughts. "I've been touching you all day."

"Not in the way I mean—not in the way I *need*." She sits up, and I fall on my ass at the end of the bed to avoid a collision. Her shirt is twisted, and her left tit is on full display.

I eye the ceiling and point. "Can you fix that?"

"See, if you wanted me, you wouldn't care if my boob was hanging out, and you certainly wouldn't look away." Her words are strong, but her voice is vulnerable in a way I haven't heard from her.

"Want has nothing to do with it." I glance and relax when I see she did cover up the nip slip. Not that I wouldn't gladly stare at her naked tits all day.

"Exactly."

She lost me while I was thinking about her naked tits. "I'm sorry, what?"

"You don't want me."

I laugh and climb off the bed. I need distance if we're going to have *that* talk. "I want you, Taylor." I pace from one side of the room to the other. "I wanted you when I was seventeen. I want you now at twenty-five." I stop and lock on her. "I've wanted you every year, every second, and every fucking breath in between. I could die tomorrow, and I'd still want you from the grave. There's no escaping it. You haunt me. Don't you see that, woman?" I grip my hair and turn away.

Fuck! Cap and Cher probably heard every word. I brace, staring at the door, expecting Cap to break it down at any second.

CHAPTER 25

O N SHAKY LEGS, I MAKE MY WAY TO HIM, HIS BACK
still to me, eyeing the door like Cam might come rushing in like he
did this morning. But he's not here, and I'm confident Cap won't
bother us. Plus, the door is locked.

"They sleep with a noise machine to block out everything except the baby monitors." I wrap around him from behind. His skin is
so warm. I want him, but I need him to know: "I can never apologize
enough for how I hurt you."

He makes a pained groan like a wounded animal. It echoes in my
soul. I tighten my embrace. How do I heal an injury this old?

"If you never want to see me again—I'll go. I'll pack up and leave
tomorrow." The thought of leaving my new family hurts, but not nearly
as much as the thought of never seeing him again. "If that's what you
need."

He turns, capturing my face. "I don't want you to leave. I'd never
ask that of you."

But is it what he needs? To never see me again? "You want me to
quit—I'll quit."

His forehead presses against mine. "No, baby. Stop offering. That's not what I want."

Relief floods me, but there's still a cavernous void between us. I grip his wrists, catching his gaze. "What do you want?"

"You." He digs his fingers into my hair, tipping my chin. Sorrowful eyes claim mine.

"I'm right here, Dually. I'm all yours. Always have been. I fear I always will be even if you never want me the way I want you, or if it's only for one night."

"One night would never be enough," he growls.

I shiver under his heated gaze and shudder a breath. "Then take me for however long you want."

Do I sound desperate? Settling? Maybe I am, but I'll take whatever he's offering.

He steps back, averting his eyes. "You were raped."

My shoulders drop. I'd hoped that wouldn't taint his opinion of me. I guess it already has. "I see." I move for my closet, feeling underdressed and entirely too vulnerable.

"Stop." He gently grips my wrist, rounding on me. "What just crossed your mind?"

I shake my head. I can't bear to look at him.

"Hey." He lowers until it's impossible to avoid him without closing my eyes. "Tell me."

"You think I'm damaged goods," I whisper, the words too heavy to hold and the grief unbearable.

I've lost him.

Again.

And I'm standing right here.

His eyes widen. "No," he protests. "I'm trying to be sensitive to your situation." Coming to his full height, he pulls me into a hug. "I don't want to hurt you, Taylor. With what you've been through, and the last twenty-four hours, I couldn't stand it if my need for you made it worse. Or made you feel pressured into doing something you're not ready for."

Can he possibly mean it? My giddy heart picks up its pace. "You want me?" I sound like a hopefully little girl who just found out her crush likes her too.

He points a few feet over where he was pacing a moment ago. "Didn't you hear my wanting-you rant?" He brackets my face, holding me steady as he leans in. "I don't want to hurt you," he reiterates.

I lift, bringing our mouths close enough to touch. My breath, the kiss I want to lay on him. "Then don't. Love me instead. Make love *to* me."

"Taylor," he cautions, but it's the most delicious of warnings.

"Don't let me go another night not remembering what it's like to be loved by you."

"Fuck," he hisses as he falls into our kiss. One lick of his tongue and my toes curl as I seal my body to his, grip his hair, and wrap my leg around his.

Nothing—and I mean *nothing*—has ever tasted as good as him or felt as devastatingly perfect.

If kisses were concertos, this one would be our masterpiece.

Pressed against my closet door, he lifts me, his fingers digging into my ass cheeks, grinding between my legs, fucking me through our clothes. I'm thrown back to spring break, the first time he kissed me, the first time he touched me, the first time he made me come, and ohmygod, the first time he slipped inside me, ending our virginity and setting unrealistic expectations for all future sexual encounters. He was my first, and despite the odds, I want him to be the last.

"Please." I claw at his back, needing to touch his skin, every inch of him bare and all mine.

"Please what, baby?" He squeezes my breasts, easily slipping past the gaping sides of my muscle shirt to twist and pull on my nipples.

Zings of pleasure ring through my body, taking my breath. "Naked. Inside me. Now."

He chuckles. "Not yet, Songbird. I need to hear you soar first."

In one fluid move, he has us across the room and on the bed, my top off and thong disposed of. I rip at his shirt, pulling it over his head before his mouth descends on my breasts. "Missed my beauties," he whispers, pressing tender kisses on each before licking and getting reacquainted.

I grind on his thigh, trying to get him closer, and unsuccessfully push his bottoms off with my heels. But when he sucks a nipple into his mouth, I lose all sanity, bowing off the bed, ready to blow if only he'd fill me up. The ache—

"Fuck. So damn wet." He slips a finger inside me. No pretense. No clit *hello*. Just going straight in, knowing what I need, pumping as he feasts on my breasts.

As I spread my legs, humping his fingers, his string of curses has me rushing to the edge. Nearly. *Ohgodsoclose.* "Landry," I plead.

"I want you to come on my cock," he growls, shoving his pants down.

Yes, yes, do that. My words don't come, yet *I* do when he rubs my clit with the tip of his cock, fingers working my insides, and his mouth on my breasts. He pins me with his body as I soar, not stopping until the last tremor works its way from head to toes with small quakes that have me shuddering.

When I finally catch my breath, his kisses head south, his mouth getting reacquainted with my most intimate places. I want to say *it's nice to see you again*, but I'm already speechless, gripping the sheets, and praying my heart doesn't explode before my body does.

Tender kisses ease her back from wherever women go when they orgasm. It must be a spectacular place with how long their orgasms can last. But with my Songbird, I'd like to think her place is me. *Me* who takes her there. *Me* who brings her home... even after all these years.

Condom on, I slide into *my* favorite place. My first heaven and hopefully my last. With languid kisses and lazy strokes, I make love to my other half for the first time in eight years. My heart splits and thumps in sorrow and joy, a breaking and a remaking, a goodbye and a hello.

I was a boy who thought he was a man the last time I was inside her. She was a woman who turned out to still be a girl. I didn't know she was only fifteen—a topic we still need to discuss. I have to believe she only lied because her heart was desperate for mine, unwilling to risk losing her soul's other half. If I were in her shoes, I would have lied without a doubt.

"Hey." She cups my cheek. "Where'd you go?"

I kiss her swollen lips, whispering, "Nowhere. Just in awe that I've found you again."

She clenches around me, sending tingles up my spine, and her nails racing up and down my back. "We still have things to talk about, but do you think we can kiss and save it for when you're not inside me?"

I kiss her nose and laugh. "So, next year sometime?"

Clench.

Fuck.

"Yes, I'll pencil you in a year from now," she teases.

I grind and change the angle of my hips. Her gasp has me increasing my speed, teasing her nipples, and kissing her deep with a hunger I now know I've only ever felt for her.

She meets me thrust for thrust, moan for moan, and desperate plea for desperate plea. When she locks her ankles behind my back, I sink in deeper, eat her cries with wanton kisses, trying to swallow her whole, nail her to the bed. Prove I'm man enough to keep her, love her, protect her.

When she comes for the third time, I silently list my high school football stats to stay my own release while praising her, thanking her, loving her.

Breathlessly, she runs her nails along my chest and abdomen. "Why didn't you... you know?"

"Come? Ejaculate? Make a deposit? Plant my seed?" I lean back on my knees, slipping out of her, my cock bobbing against my stomach.

Her flush deepens as she eyes my glistening erection. Her embarrassment is sexy as fuck. "Yeah, that."

I hover over my Heartbreaker, needing to be sure of one thing. "Are you okay?" I was a little lost in her pleasure to be sure she's as good as I need her to be.

She runs her thumb along the head of my cock, making it jump in need as she bites her bottom lip. "I'm perfect. But I'd be even better if you stopped worrying and let go."

"I will. I just needed to be sure." I pat her thigh. "Flip over, ass up."

Her eyes widen. "W-why?"

Now she's shy? "It'll feel amazing, promise." I kiss down her neck to her ripe breasts that are larger than they were and even more spectacular.

When she's squirming below me, turned on nearly as much as me, I get her to her side and fill her in one long stroke.

Her gasps and moans are everything as I pick up the pace, gripping her top leg and thrusting as far as I can get before retreating. Over and over.

"Landry." She grips my arm, using it for leverage to push her hips into me, faster and faster as our need grows.

I slide my hand down her stomach to rub her clit. "You gonna come for me, Songbird?"

"Yes," she mewls. "Ohmygodyes."

"That's it, beautiful." Fuck. She squeezes me so damn perfectly. I couldn't hold back even if I tried. Warmth that starts in my gut fills me as her green eyes lock on mine. *I'm going to love you forever* is on the tip of my tongue as she comes and takes me with her.

I lost my sentimentality eight years ago. I guess she found it and brought it back to me.

With her cleaned up and curled into my side a while later, I make a vow to do whatever is necessary to keep her. Not losing her this time.

"Taylor," I breathe into her hair. "I'm sorry I've been an ass. Do you think we can move forward from here? Forgive our younger selves for how things ended between us?"

Wide eyes meet my worried gaze. "Are you serious? Just forgive and forget?" She rests her chin on my chest. "Also, you really were an ass. The way you treated me really hurt."

I hear her unasked question: *How do I know you won't do it again?*

Sweeping her hair over her shoulder, I'm struck by how much she's the same beauty she was at fifteen, yet even more so now. She's been through so much. "I never want to be the cause of your pain. My anger over the past clouded my perspective. I'm coming to accept you didn't control your world back then. The mistakes I made were my own. You hurt me, but my reaction to that hurt then and now are on me. You were fifteen, nearly sixteen. I was barely seventeen. What did either of us know about forever? There's a high probability we would have crashed and burned. I'd rather have a second chance with you now than have burned up my chances back then."

"You knew? About my age?"

I shake my head. "I found out yesterday. That's why I let Ruby and that other woman flirt with me. I wanted to hurt you for lying to me, for making me feel like I didn't really know you at all, when deep down I know I do. Everything I believed to be true about how things ended, and now how we began, felt like lies on top of lies. You keep rocking my world, and I keep stumbling, trying to keep up." My eyes prick with emotions I fight to keep in check. Reconciling old hurts with new truths is hard.

"There's only one way I want to rock your world." She lifts, sliding across me until she's straddling my hardening cock. "I can't express how sorry I am or how alone I felt after I left you. And I shouldn't have lied about my age, but I didn't think you'd give me a second glance if you knew. It doesn't excuse the lie, only explains it." She leans forward, her hands splayed across my chest. "Can you forgive me?" A wave of uncertainty washes across her face.

I cup her cheek, gripping her hip to still her slow gyrations. "Forgiven, baby." I slip my hand into her hair, gently urging her forward. "Now kiss me and show me how you rule my world."

Her smile is sexy and devious, lighting up her eyes as she closes the distance, whispering, "Forgiven," across my lips before she seals her mouth to mine.

She's mine, and I'm not letting anyone get in the way of that.

Not even me.

CHAPTER 26

MY PALM SLAPS AGAINST THE COOL SHOWER TILE, and I twist my mouth, locking my moan inside instead of letting it reverberate off the bathroom walls. Cap and Cher's room is entirely too close. Thankfully, I'm pretty sure they're downstairs.

"Fuck, Songbird," he growls next to my ear. "You feel so good." His grip on my hips tightens, setting off zings of pleasure. "Too good."

Yes. My head falls forward, and I push back, needing him deeper, harder, faster. When he does, I can't hold back; I open my mouth to get more air, and a slow moan escapes instead.

He slams into me, leaning forward, his front pressed to my back, and wraps an arm around my chest, cupping and kneading my breast. His other hand brackets mine on the wall. He twists my nipple. "Do you want my hand on your breasts or your clit?" His ragged words skate along my neck, sending cascades of goosebumps down my arms.

Holymotherfullofgracebothplease. I can't answer, yet he seems to know. Pulling me back, he pins me to his chest. Both arms circle my body: one on my breasts, the other tight on my abdomen with his fingers skimming my clit with each thrust. My feet barely touch the shower floor as he drills into me, murmuring dirty praise in my ear.

I didn't know I was a praise slut until his words rain down on me, sliding along my sensitized skin, leaving his invisible mark, petting my self-esteem, and amping up my need for him.

The tingles begin in my toes, teasing upwards, flexing each muscle, bowing me back, me head hitting his shoulder as I silently scream his name and come, jerking in his arms.

He holds me, kissing my neck, growling my name as he fills me.

And fills me.

And fills me.

I love the no-condom decision. Actually *feeling* his release is a heady experience and draws out my pleasure with small spasms like mini earthquakes, shattering the last barrier surrounding my heart and the tight grip I have on my emotions. I nearly crumble to the shower floor before he catches me, turning me around to find I'm an emotional wreck. The dam has broken.

"Baby." He pulls me into his chest, kissing my head, trying to soothe me. "Did I hurt you?" The trepidation in his voice only makes it worse.

"No," I croak. This time with him has been spectacular. If I thought sex with him when we were kids was the best of my life, then this must be the afterlife because I can barely stand after all the life-altering sex we've had. I haven't been with many guys since him. It took me a while to even want to try with anyone else, and the results didn't inspire me to try harder. They were *fine*. Sex was *okay*. I rarely came. They rarely noticed. The fact that Landry actively wants me to come—multiple times—before he even considers finding his own release, is a hard pill to swallow. I was so close to never finding this again—never finding him.

I don't want to lose him. Not because of the sex, but yes, *also* because of the sex.

The tears won't stop.

All the years wasted.

We could have been an established family by now.

I never would have been in that car, driving solo to Vegas. I never would have met Beau. Never would have been—

"Hey, hey." Landry brings my face into view, his eyes searching mine. "What's going on?"

I shake my head and bury my face in his neck. "Hold me, please."

"Always." He punches out a breath and tightens his embrace. "Need to get you dried off. You're shaking."

I'm not shaking because I'm cold.

He quickly rinses us off. I had already washed my hair before he surprised me by slipping in the shower to wish me *good morning*. Now, he probably thinks I'm crazy... Or worse, broken.

Wrapped in towels, we traipse across the hall to my room. I don't even glance to see if anyone spots us. I don't really care. In my room, he brushes and clips my hair up like he's been doing it for years, kisses my shoulder and holds open my robe for me to slip into.

"I don't think you should go to work." He cups my cheek after I'm all wrapped up. "You need to rest."

Would he stay with me? I'm sure he would if I asked, but he needs to go to the gym to train, and his business needs him. He's the boss. "I'm fine." I kiss the palm of his hand. "I was overwhelmed with emotions. That's all."

His scowl isn't convinced. "Let me feed you and then see how you're doing."

He gets me settled on the bed with the TV remote and goes in search of food. I don't mind him taking care of me. I don't mind it one bit.

Cap is in the kitchen talking to a couple of beefy guys and one rather petite woman. He spots me over their shoulders. "Landry, come meet Taylor's security detail."

I'm glad I threw on my jeans and a t-shirt rather than tumble down the stairs in just pajama bottoms and nothing else. Cap introduces me to Brady, the biggest of the bunch, then Rick, who holds his own in the size department. The little firecracker is Ramona. She nearly breaks my hand with her kung-fu-grip handshake. She has a point to make, clearly.

"It's nice to meet y'all." I eye Cap and them. "Who's sticking to Taylor, and who's working at my bar?"

"We'll trade off the mornings following her from home to the bakery or anywhere else she goes. We'll all be working at Mel's while Ms. Permian-O'Dair is there," Brady offers. He must be in charge. He hands me a card with their numbers on it.

"Ms. Permian-O'Dair is—"

"Right here." Taylor saunters into the kitchen all fresh and lovely in cutoffs and a Sugarplum's t-shirt, not a hint of the emotional mess she was only minutes ago, except maybe the red tip of her cute nose. "And please call me Taylor. It'll make working together easier at Mel's. No slip-ups calling me Ms. *Whatever.*"

As is usual at Cap's, breakfast is ready and waiting. I dish up Taylor's plate as introductions are exchanged and a repeat of who's working where. When she has them enthralled and answering personal questions she doesn't need to know about them, I pull her to the table and kiss her head. "You need to eat."

"You'll join me, won't you?" She grabs my hand before I get too far, worry shimmering in her green eyes. She's not as okay as she wants everyone to believe.

I see you, baby.

I don't miss everyone focusing on us as I bend to kiss her softly. "Not going anywhere, Songbird. Just getting some food."

After we've eaten and Taylor heads upstairs to brush her teeth and get her things to leave for the bakery, Cap comes to stand shoulder-to-shoulder as I stare up the stairs.

"She's not okay, is she?"

I shake my head. "Not even a little. But I can't convince her to stay home and let me coddle her. She wants to stay busy, not let that asshole run her life, box her in. She's right, I guess, but…"

"What about you?" He nudges me. "You doing okay?"

"I want to rip his head off." Not even joking. "But, yeah, I'm happy to have her back."

His brow arches. "Back, huh? Someday you'll fill me in?"

I nod up the stairs as the girl of my dreams heads our way. "*She'll* fill you in." I pat his back, whispering, "When she's ready," seconds before she jumps in my arms. I manage to hold us upright and carry her to her car. She insists on driving. I want to take her, but I know she needs to do this. Own her path. Brady will be shadowing her, keeping her safe.

I pray he does, or he'll have me to reckon with.

CHAPTER 27

I HAVEN'T SLEPT IN MY BED IN WEEKS, AND I'M pleased as fuck about it. I've been staying at Cap's with my girl, and he's being extremely cool about it. Taylor isn't a teenager, but still, many parents wouldn't be okay with their kid's boyfriend or girlfriend staying over *in* their kid's room. I'd rather Taylor was at my place or we found our own, but I don't want to push for more too soon. She's walking on eggshells, afraid of what's around the corner that could jeopardize what we have.

Plus, it's safer at Cap's where he can keep an eye on her when I'm not around. Even though we have security in place, I feel better knowing Cap is never more than a room away when she's home. He's been working from home more and more if either Cher or Taylor will be there. Cher has started working again but with reduced hours, easing into her new schedule after being off for months after having Iris. Maybe Taylor would like being around her new family for a bit, even in better circumstances, soak up some love.

Now, if we can just catch this asshole stalking my girl, we'd be all good.

The visual of what he did to Taylor spurs my kick into Rowdy's side, knocking him off balance.

"Fuck, you put a little heat on that one. Is that how we're doin' this? You want to go full out, Cowboy?" Rowdy circles the ring.

I shouldn't say *yes*, but I can see it in his eyes, the need to tip the edge, maybe not all out, but more than he's been holding back to help me with my training. "Bring it."

"No," Jonah barks from the other side of the ropes. "Don't fucking bring it, Rowdy. Save it for fight night!"

Gabriel just laughs and offers a chin nod of approval.

I wiggle my shoulders and crack my neck, letting my anger flow. "I've got one word for you, Rowdy... Beau."

In a snap, he's on me, and it's fight night after all.

He jabs left. I duck right, followed by an elbow strike that lands right where I intended. Like an idiot, I gloat instead of paying attention and take a knee to the ribs and a kick to the shin.

"Oomph," Jonah hisses.

"Maybe not all out," Gabriel warns from the ropes. I'm not sure if he's talking to me or Rowdy, but given I'm the one limping, I'm pretty sure it's not me.

In my periphery, Walker, Sloan, and Patrick amble over to watch the spectacle. I don't want to get hurt or hurt Rowdy, but I can't let him one-up me. I respect the guy, and he is Taylor's brother and Cap's son, but I'm still not holding back.

In a move Gabriel taught me when I first started sparring with him, I fake left, dart right, taking a shot to the jaw but use the momentum to land a hook to his side, the same spot I kicked a minute ago, followed by a knee, and take him down with a leg sweep. Rowdy falls like the giant he is, though he's only a few inches taller than me.

The guys whistle and whoop, egging us on.

Jonah, ever the voice of reason, demands, "Enough! Landry, get out of the ring before Rowdy hurts you."

"Me?" I point at the man getting up. "Who's on the floor?"

"*You*, when I get my hands on you," Rowdy seethes.

"Whoa." Gabriel gets in Rowdy's eye-line. "Calm down. This is the guy who loves your sister."

"Stop. I don't need you to protect me. And thanks for the vote of confidence, by the way." I scowl at Gabriel.

"He's sleeping with my sister," Rowdy rasps, breathing hard and oozing menace.

Wait. He's supposed to be pissed about Beau. Not me.

"Oh, he's doing more than *sleeping* with her." Walker throws lighter fluid on an already too hot flame.

I glare at Walker. "Shut the fuck up. You don't talk about Taylor like that." I point at all of them. "None of you get to talk shit about her. Understand?"

They grumble their assent. Rowdy clocks me across the nose and cheek, taking advantage of my distracted state.

"Fuck!" I stumble back, gripping the rope to stay standing and breathe through the pain as blood gushes from my nose. "You broke my fucking nose!"

"How do you really know my sister?!" Rowdy is in my face, not giving a shit about injuring a teammate and friend.

In a flash Gabriel has Rowdy pinned to the floor, face down, his arm bent behind his back. Rowdy grunts, but doesn't cede, his heated gaze still on me.

"You want to talk about sisters?" Gabriel bends Rowdy's arm to an unnatural angle. "Then let's talk."

"You approved of me dating Reese. I'm fucking married to her with a kid. It's too fucking late to make a stink now," Rowdy grits through clenched teeth.

"And you approved of Landry dating Taylor when you thought it was newer than it is. How they met doesn't fucking matter. The fact that they love each other and he would lay down his life for her is all that fucking matters. It should matter more that he *still* cares about her." He eases up on Rowdy's arm, waiting a moment before letting go but pressing his knee to Rowdy's back. "You gonna calm down, or do you need to fight it out with *me?*" Gabriel is not being an ass. He's offering Rowdy an outlet for his pent-up anger, offering himself as a human punching bag.

And just like that, Rowdy's rage is gone. "She was…." His anguish is palpable. *Raped.* He doesn't finish the thought, thankfully. She wouldn't want everyone knowing her business.

I drop to my knees beside him, my head bowed, the depth of his anguish ringing true in me. "We'll fucking get him, Cam. He'll pay for what he did." It'll never erase what happened to her, but it's a start at moving forward. I stand and offer him my hand. "If you need to hit me again, you can."

On his feet, Rowdy snags his towel from the corner, handing it to me. "Sorry about your nose."

I shrug it off. "Not my first and probably not my last broken nose. But I should pop it back in place and get some ice on it. Your sister's not going to be thrilled when she sees me slightly less pretty…"

He flinches. "Yeah, I doubt she'll be too happy with me."

"It was a training accident. We left it on the mat." I hop the ropes and make my way to the locker room.

"I'll get you some ice," Gabriel offers.

"I'll get you some Advil." Jonah scowls at the big man. "I could have gotten the ice."

Gabriel shrugs. "Now you don't have to."

I leave them bickering on the other side of the locker room door and start stripping to hit the showers. I could've lasted a few more hours, but now I feel wiped and need to see Taylor. Be sure she's alright, spend a little time together before we head to the bar tonight.

"Hey," Rowdy's voice pulls me from my thoughts. "I really am sorry. I shouldn't have been sparring with you or anyone until that scumbag is caught. I'm on edge and shouldn't have taken it out on you. Pain transmission, pure and simple."

I turn on the shower, letting the cool water hit my back before it starts to warm. "I understand." I bracket my nose with my hands and swiftly pop it back into place. I see stars for a second but blink through the tears. "Really. I'm good." I turn, facing the wall, bending my head and letting the water wash over my hair and face, watching the blood fade as it circles the drain.

Just another day in the life of a fighter.

Shit, I'm gonna have two black eyes later.

I hope Taylor likes raccoons.

CHAPTER 28

MY SMILE CAN'T BE HELPED WHEN I FIND LANDRY'S truck in the driveway upon returning home from Cher's bakery to get ready for work at Mel's. Though I don't want to take the time, I pull into the third space in the garage so I don't block the driveway for Cher or Cap when they get home. Plus, those extra thirty seconds aren't going to kill me.

The ridiculous thought has me looking around the space before I turn off my engine and close the garage. *Beau is not in here.* He wouldn't be that stupid or that clever, right?

When I don't find Landry in the main part of the house, I head upstairs to find him asleep on my bed in only his boxer briefs and an ice pack on his face. That can't be good. I peer over the ice pack, trying to be stealthy and not wake him. I can't really see much, maybe a little purpling on his eyelids, but it could be shadows from the darkened room.

My phone vibrates in my pocket. I venture to the bench at the end of the bed and check my phone.

Cameron: *I'm sorry about Landry's face. I fucked up.*

What the hell?

Me: *You did this? What happened?*

Cameron: *We were sparring. Things got heated. It's my fault. Be mad at me.*

I wasn't considering being mad at *anyone*. They're fighters. Injuries are bound to happen. But…

Me: *Did you mean to hurt him?*

Cameron: *I'd rather not answer that.*

OMG. What?!

Me: *You're an idiot.*

Cameron: *Agreed.*

Wow. Cam admitting guilt is not something I typically witness. Though we have had tender moments, when it comes to me, he leans more toward the I'm-your-big-brother-hear-me-roar kind of attitude.

Me: *Did you apologize?*

Cameron: *Yes.*

Me: *Then it's for him to forgive.*

Seconds later, I'm wrapped in strong, familiar arms and tossed on the bed. My phone is forgotten as Landry's heated gaze traverses my body before locking on my face. "Sorry I fell asleep." He hovers over me, his longer hair on top hanging low, nearly covering his eyes.

I sweep my fingers through it, holding it captive as I study his injuries. He has the makings of two black eyes, swelling and bruising along his puffy nose. "Did he break it?"

Landry sighs and drops to his back. "He did." There's no anger in his words.

Rolling to my side, propped on my elbow, I run a finger along his jaw. "You need anything?"

"Kiss it and make it better." The edge to his voice sends chills along my spine. I lean in and barely kiss the tip. He shakes his head. "That's not where I need your kisses."

I pop a brow, trying to hide my smile. He's playful so must not be hurting too badly. "Really? And where do you need me to kiss to make it all betters?"

"Here." He points to the impressive bulge in his briefs. "I need your lips all over me, Songbird."

By the time I get my bedroom door locked and turn around, he's naked on the bed. His *I need kisses* hard-on is saluting me. I wonder how long he can last with only kisses? I strip on my way to the bed. He loves to command me, but I love his hands on me even more than his words.

I start slow. A teasing kiss to his lips, followed by licks and sucks as I move down his neck to his pecs. I get a zing of pleasure when he hisses over getting his nipples sucked. I moan and rub against his thigh when he tweaks my nipples as I play with his.

"You'll make me come if you keep that up," I mumble against his tight little peak.

He grips my ass and moves so I'm straddling his cock, grinding me against his hard length. "I'm not complaining about that, baby. Not one bit." His hand slips into my hair, bringing my mouth to meet his in a scorching kiss.

By the time he breaks the kiss, I'm a sloppy mess on his lap, and he's slipping inside me.

"I thought you wanted my mouth," I halfheartedly protest. I mean, his cock inside me is mutually beneficial. But his growliness when I have him in my mouth shouldn't be easily dismissed either.

"Changed my mind, baby. Need you now." He surges up while holding me down by my hips.

His grip is not gentle, and I love every second of it. Spurring me forward, I ride him like the horses I never did learn how to ride, which is not unusual for city folk. Most Texans don't grow up on horses.

My hand splayed on his chest, I squeeze his pecs and run my thumbs along his nipples. His moan of approval hardens my nips and doesn't go unnoticed. Landry squeezes my breasts, twisting and pulling on my peaks before capturing a tight bud in his mouth and sucking deeply. He slips his other hand low on my belly, splayed out with his thumb circling my clit. He uses his free hand to grip my ass, guiding me into each thrust.

I grab the headboard and ram into him with a fierceness that will either have him puncturing my cervix or will take us both to the edge of ecstasy. A few rough thrusts and he growls, "You need to come, Songbird. Fucking sing for me."

His desire is my wish.

His need is my sustenance.

His pleasure is my sanity.

Rocking. Rocking. Rocking. I come in a split second between living and fearing death, catapulting to the furthest realm in my mind between heaven and the hell of never feeling this again, living in the innocence of our first time and the greedy hunger of this time.

It is the little death, reminding me of how fragile life is and how resilient our bodies are, able to withstand so much pain and endless pleasure.

"Taylor," he growls, locking me in his embrace, grinding against me, in me, through me as we come and come and come.

Hours later, after I perform, and just before he's supposed to be on stage, I drop to my knees in his office and kiss him all better from tip to base, from balls to taint and every inch in between as far as I can take him.

And take him.

And take him.

Just when I think he's about to come, he pulls me to my feet, bending me over his desk, pulling down my shorts and panties with a quick love bite to my ass. "Not coming without you, baby."

He drills me from behind, covering my smiling mouth with his hand as his desk gives way to his demanding thrusts and starts to scoot across the floor. "Fuck, you make me so crazy, Taylor. I can't get deep enough."

"You feel pretty deep to me," I mumble around his hand.

He stops. Panting, he leans down, capturing my face. "Am I hurting you?"

The concern in his eyes and on his handsome face have my eyes prickling. I kiss his cheek and push back, taking him deeper. "Only in the best of ways, Dually."

"Fuck, why do I love that stupid nickname?" He picks up the pace.

"Because it reminds you of me before I broke us." My voice hitches, and I grip the desk, fighting to keep my emotions at bay.

Why do I keep crying during sex? What the hell is wrong with me? Just when I think I've put it all behind me, our past comes bubbling up to wreak havoc on the moment.

"Taylor?" He pulls out completely.

"No," I groan. I'm messing this all up.

"Hey, it's okay." He kisses me soundly when he turns me and sets me on the edge of his desk, pulling off my left boot to get my leg free of my shorts and panties. Then he surges inside, leaning over, forcing me to lie back.

His pace is slower but no less devastating. I try to hide in his neck, but he's not having it. "I need your eyes, Taylor. I need to know you're alright."

"I don't want you to see me cry and stop." *I don't want to be this vulnerable, this desperate for your love.* "I'm crying, but I *need* this."

He tips my chin, pressing his lips to mine before meeting my gaze. "Cry, laugh, scream. Do whatever you need to do, whatever feels right. I want you in whatever state of mind you're in."

"That sounds like a song."

He smiles. "It could be."

Our kiss is more tender as he starts to move. His thumb is on my clit, making me shake and tremble, working my way up the stream, against the current, in hopes of reaching the top of the dam and riding the waves all the way down—with him.

Leo knocks on the door. "The band is waiting."

Landry barks, "I'm coming. Tell them to hold their fucking horses."

If Leo replies, I don't hear it over the heat in Landry's eyes and the added pressure on my clit. "You gonna come all over my cock, Songbird?"

Yes, I nod and bite my lip, nipples tingling with want but no time for them to get the attention they need.

"—squeeze me so good, I nearly lose my mind with the need to spill inside you."

Ohmygodplease.

He sucks my bottom lip to free it. "When we get home, I'm going to fuck your mouth till I come down your throat, then eat this sweet pussy till you're begging to feel me deep inside you."

Landry's dirty talk is on point and exactly what I need to get me *there*.

I clench around him, and he grabs my breast over my Mel's Bar t-shirt. "Never going to stop loving you, Taylor."

"Landry." My body vibrates, ringing out from the chord he masterfully struck.

"There's my girl." He smashes his mouth to mine, drilling me with his tongue as he drills me with his cock. Groaning and swearing, he releases with me.

"I love you, Landry. Always have. Always will," I finally admit.

For a second, I swear I hear chimes. Like we reach a new level of intimacy and heaven is celebrating. How silly is that?

"Love you, Songbird. All my life."

CHAPTER 29

"**Y**OU READY?" I STEAL ONE LAST KISS BEFORE opening my office door. Outside of family who already know, we've been keeping our relationship on the downlow. Leo walked in on us kissing last week before everyone else arrived. Others suspect, but no one has asked, and I'd like to keep it that way until her stalker is caught, and she ready to be open about us.

She's under a microscope since her panic attack a few weeks ago and the influx of security people pretending to be new employees, who watch her like a hawk, which is their job. I'm lucky she works here. If she were at a law firm, it wouldn't be so easy to plant new "employees."

Understandably, she doesn't want to bring any more attention to herself by also dating the boss. That position will be harder on her than me. I want to scream it from the rooftops, but I understand her want to legitimize herself for her skills before revealing she's got an inside connection to the place. But really, it's a fucking bar. What perks are there? Free alcohol she rarely drinks? A singing gig she could have landed nearly anywhere in this town? Sex at work? Well, yes, that one is a true perk, I'm happy to say.

"Yep. They're going to wonder where you are." She casts a worrisome brow toward me.

"I'm the boss. They go on when I say." One more kiss. "I just hope they're not too drunk to play."

She's laughing as I open the door, and she steps out.

"What the hell?!"

I stop short, gripping Taylor by the hip, bringing her back to my front as I glare over her head at Ruby. "Watch it," I warn. I've had about all I can take of Ruby and her antics to get at my junk. My junk solely belongs to my Heartbreaker.

"Watch it?!" she screeches. "You won't fuck me, but you'll fuck her?!" She jabs a pointy-nailed finger in Taylor's shoulder before I can stop her.

Taylor shoves her back. "You should watch the way you talk to your boss, Ruby. Especially when you don't know what you're talking about."

I didn't need to worry. I cross my arms, try not to smile, and watch my girl put Ruby in her place. I don't mind her claiming me in the meantime one bit.

Ruby is only stunned for a second before she steps forward. "You won't last. I'll be fucking him next."

"Enough!" I bark, placing my hand on Taylor's arm, nudging her aside, needing to protect her from Ruby's lies and empty threats.

My girl's possessive green glare flashes to me, flattening her palm on my chest and blocking me from getting in front of her. "Listen up, *Rubes*, as I'm only going to say this one time." She leans in, getting in Ruby's face. "I was his *first*, and I will be his *last*. You can sell your skank-ass wares somewhere else."

"His first?"

My head whips to the side, finding Rowdy and Gabriel blocking the end of the hall. "Shit." I forgot they were here. I should have known they'd come running with any sign of trouble.

"Cam," Taylor gasps, falling back a step before getting herself together and marching toward her brother. "Don't." She points at him. "Don't say a word!"

Gabriel pulls Ruby out of the way and eyes me speculatively. "Why don't we take this to the office or out back?"

"Out back." I grab Taylor's hand and pull her with me out the back door, not giving a shit if Rowdy follows. But, of course, he does.

Taylor is on him the second I release her hand, pushing at his chest. "Cam, stop. Please don't say another word! Let me talk to him first."

He ignores his sister's protest, stepping aside, and heads straight for me, anger rippling off his body. "You—"

"Stop." Gabriel steps in to stop him. "This is between the two of them, don'tcha think?"

"Look." I raise my hands. I have no intention of fighting Rowdy. We already did that, and I have the broken nose to prove it. "I love your sister. She loves me."

"You—" Rowdy barrels past Gabriel. "You're the asshole who took her virginity and knocked her up!"

"What?" My stomach drops, and my heart picks up its pace. "Taylor?"

"No, please," she cries, trying to push Rowdy back as Gabriel gets him in a choke hold, and I finally understand why she seemed so desperate a moment ago.

"Taylor!" I bark. "What is he saying?"

She steps to me, but I back up, holding my hand out. "Don't touch me." The ground is shaking below my feet, and if I fall, I might just take her with me. "Say it."

"Please," she begs. "Landry, I never wanted you to find out this way."

I lean against whoever's car I back into, needing the support.

"Tell him," Gabriel commands before he whispers in Rowdy's ear things I can't hear, and I should probably be happy I can't, but there are too many secrets flying around as it is.

"Remember I told you my older brother Drake came to Padre and literally dragged me away." She points over her shoulder. "Cam had to leave too because he was in trouble for not keeping a better eye on me. He didn't know about you. None of them did until—" She breaks down into a sob, falling to her knees.

"Let me go," Rowdy growls, tapping Gabriel's arm. "Taylor needs me. I won't touch him."

"Until what?" I latch on to Gabriel's arm when he comes to stand beside me. *Please don't say it.*

My Heartbreaker rocks on the gravel beneath her, shaking her head. "I'm so sorry. I'm so sorry. I'm so sorry," she mumbles.

Rowdy squats beside her, gently touching her shoulder.

Instinctually, I move to comfort her, but stop. "Until what, Taylor?"

On a stuttered breath, she whimpers, "Until I found out I was pregnant a few weeks later."

Fuck. Me. I stumble back, falling on my ass, my head whirling. "You left me, ghosted me, and were pregnant with my kid?" I grip my hair. Maybe if I tug hard enough, I'll wake up, and all of this will be a dream. We'll be asleep on my office couch, none the wiser, sated in finally admitting our renewed love for each other.

But, no. Here we are in the back of my bar, and I'm having my guts ripped out by my Heartbreaker all over again.

The more things change, the more they stay the fucking same.

"Where's my child now? Do I have a s-son or daughter?" I stagger to my feet, ready to go find him or her before he or she goes a second longer believing they're not wanted. I know what that feels like. Taylor may not have wanted our baby, but I sure as fuck do. I want my family.

She shakes her head, tears streaming down her face, pleading with me to make it stop.

Yeah, baby, make it stop.

"Tell. Me." I step forward.

Rowdy moves in front of Taylor.

Just as fast, Gabriel is in front of me. "Tell him," he implores. "He deserves to hear it all."

When it looks like Taylor can't form a coherent phrase, Rowdy bends and picks her up just as Reese and Frankie come flying out the back door, shuffling to a stop at the scene before them.

Rowdy whispers something to Taylor, who nods. He takes a long breath and releases it just as slowly. "She miscarried around ten weeks." He shakes his head. "There is no kid." He turns and walks away with my Heartbreaker in his arms, slowing for Reese to join him. She flicks a sad smile over her shoulder.

"She left her guitar and purse. She'll want them," I mutter as I stumble to my car. I don't know where I'm going. I live here, above my fucking bar. Most of my clothes are at Cap's, and my main reason for living all these years was just carried off by her brother, who no doubt hates me.

I hate me.

And as much as I want to hate Taylor, I can't. I'm angry as fuck.

And she was just a kid—fucking fifteen years old. Pregnant by a spring break fling. I thought I loved her enough for the both of us. For the first time, I think I might be wrong on all counts.

I left her pregnant.

We were careful.

Fuck, we were only kids, obviously not careful enough.

I had a kid. For ten weeks I was going to be a father. I clutch my chest, tears falling.

I left her alone to deal with it. I should've tried harder to find her. But how? I only had her first name and the city she lived in.

All these years she's carried that grief. All these years I've been pissed at being left behind. How lonely she must have felt, and now she's dealing with an asshole stalker.

Not just a stalker, a man who already...

I'm an idiot. She should be the one mad at me, then and now.

I've been harboring anger.

She's been harboring grief.

I've felt abandoned.

I've abandoned her.

Gabriel stops me. "Come to our house. Don't drive like this. Let me take you." He holds out his hand, waiting. "Don't make this night worse by dying in a car accident."

I drop the keys in his hand as a humorless laugh bubbles out. "Dying just might have my night looking up." I open my passenger door and climb in, throw my head back and close my eyes.

I thought losing my Heartbreaker at seventeen was bad. Nothing could compare to this.

CHAPTER 30

THERE WAS A SMALL PART OF ME THAT BELIEVED freeing the secrets of my past would be cathartic. That part of me is an idiot and so very wrong. I feel anything but lighter, freed, or cleansed. Cam can barely look at me.

His obligation to *look out for me* is a penance he's not too thrilled with at the moment. After depositing me in his truck's back seat, he went back for my purse and guitar. Silently, Reese climbed in the back and held me on the way to Cap's. She's a quiet person to begin with, but I'm sure my issues have dredged up pieces of her past she'd hoped would stay there. I don't know all of her story, and I don't know if she knows mine, but I'm sure she'll be getting an earful from my brother tonight.

As soon as he parks in Cap's driveway, I hop out with a murmured, "Thank you," to Reese. I make it to the front door before remembering my stuff. Turning, I nearly run into Cam. He has my guitar and purse. I unlock the door and try to take my things from him.

"I got it," he grumbles and sidesteps me, placing my things in the entryway.

Cap rushes down the stairs with Cher close behind. "Taylor." He pulls me in for a hug that's all too comforting and safe. "What happened? Frankie called and said Rowdy was bringing you home."

I pull away before my emotions have me breaking down again. Before I can answer, Cam slips in to greet Cap and Cher, then heads for the exit. I guess he's not sticking around. One foot out the door, he pauses, runs his fingers through his hair and has what appears to be a silent conversation with his wife through the car window. Reese's eyes flash to me before she flicks a heated glare in his direction.

Cam's shoulders fall as he turns, his eyes widening when he finds my gaze already on him. "I'm sorry about tonight. I didn't see it from either of your perspectives. I just need time to process." He kisses my head with a quick squeeze of my hand. "I love you, Tay." Then he's gone before I can formulate any words because I'm still lost in his *I'm sorry*.

Cher eases me to the side so she can close and lock the door. "I think I'm in shock," I mutter. "Everything was so perfect right up until… Cam had to open his big mouth. Why was he even there? He broke Landry's nose earlier, then comes in like a bulldozer sticking his nose where it doesn't belong. He had no right!" I look up to find Cher and Cap watching me, concern written all over their faces, holding hands like the amazing #couplegoals they are.

They both open their arms—one each—inviting me in for a group hug. My heart hurts. "I can't." I pass them and head for the kitchen. "If I start crying now, I'll never stop. A hug is an invitation I can't accept."

"Sit." Cap directs me to a bar stool on the other side of the island.

"How about some pancakes?" Cher asks.

"I'm really not hungry."

"Nachos?" Cap offers.

Now, that sounds good. "I could do nachos."

Cher fills some glasses with ice and sets one next to me with a Dr. Pepper. "I haven't had a DP in forever."

She smiles. "I know. You mentioned it the other day, so I grabbed some at the store. I haven't had one since I was a kid. I'm having one too."

Dang, she's always too sweet to me. "Thanks." I pop the can and take a soothing breath when I pour it into the glass. The sizzle of the carbonation hitting the air is other-level sensory goodness, reminding me of better times, of childhood, and playing outside during the summer or weekends, before things got complicated with boys and sex.

"Tell us how you met Landry," Cap prompts.

I'm not even surprised he knows that much. He's intuitive. "I guess we didn't do a great job at hiding the fact we knew each other from before Cam's wedding."

He shrugs, working on grating cheese as Cher slathers refried beans on tortilla chips. "I don't think everyone noticed. I was watching you closely, as it was the first time we'd met. Yet you were mine, and I couldn't treat you like I knew." His smile is sweet if not a little sad. "You reminded me so much of your mom—all the things I loved about her."

Cher smiles up at him, giving him a soft nudge on the arm with her head as their hands remain busy. He kisses the top of her head, lingering for a moment with his eyes closed.

I have to look away. Their love is palpable and painful to witness in light of how badly my love life has crashed and burned. "I met him on spring break. He was seventeen. I was nearly sixteen, but I lied—told him I was seventeen too…"

Once I start talking, I don't stop, not until the bitter end of how tonight went down.

Through it all, they remain silent, the nachos long forgotten on the counter, my eyes focusing anywhere but on them, swiping at my tears as they fall in a steady stream. I don't break down. I manage to keep it together. I guess that's something to be proud of. God knows there's not much else.

"Taylor, honey." Cher grips my hand resting on the island. "My situation was totally different, but I had Gabriel at sixteen. I know how scary that can be. I'm so sorry for your loss, your heartache." She comes around the counter to stand next to me. "Landry is a good man. He loves you. He just needs time. Tonight, he found out he lost more than just you when he was seventeen. Give him the grace to process it and be open when he's ready to talk."

She glances at Cap. "You need to talk to him, reassure him that he hasn't lost his place as a fighter on your team, in our family. He's lost so much in Taylor, but now he's coping with the possibility of losing Rowdy as a friend and you as a boss, mentor, father figure. He's all alone."

God, I hadn't thought of that. As messed up as my family life was, I at least had them as support then and now.

Cap nods. "He's with Gabriel. But, yeah, I'll talk to him. He's not going anywhere. He didn't do anything wrong, despite how Rowdy made him feel."

I meet Cap's gaze over the island. "I don't want to lose him. But if it's too hard for him with me being here, I can go home." I shrug, playing with the edge of the counter. "Or somewhere else." I don't know how I'll afford it, but I'm willing to leave if that's what he needs. I can't mess up his life here. He has Mel's, his friends, his family, and his fighting career. I can't be the reason he loses one more thing.

I'm in Cap's arms before my next breath. "You're not going anywhere. I just got you." His voice breaking has my tears falling faster. "I'm not losing you. I'm not losing Landry." He pulls Cher into our hug. "I've finally got my family all together. Nobody's going fucking anywhere."

CHAPTER 31

'VE LOST TRACK OF TIME, SITTING ON GABRIEL'S BACK porch as Gabriel and Frankie see to their babysitter, check on Ox, and do whatever married couples do before dealing with my sorry ass.

Though I'm technically in training for my fight coming up in a week, Gabriel offered me a bottle of Jack. I turned him down, deciding on a couple of juice boxes instead. I'm a baller like that.

I text with Leo to be sure Mel's is covered. He needs a raise. I need to hire another manager to help out, take on more, so I don't have to work till three in the morning, though Leo would do it. He needs time off too, either come in later or leave earlier.

The back door opens, and Gabriel leans out. "You don't need to hide out here. Come inside. Ox is down, and Frankie is heading to bed."

"I'm sorry your night out got jacked." I amble past him, tossing my empty boxes in the trash.

He laughs. "No apology needed. We are where we're needed. You sure you don't want anything stronger?"

"Nah, my old man and grandfather drank their sorrows away—or they tried. I've no intention of dancing that line anymore."

"I didn't know, man."

"Yeah, I don't talk about it much. They're gone anyway. Ironically killed by a drunk driver on their way to an AA meeting. Found out on my eighteen birthday."

"Damn. Sorry." He heads for the fridge, grabbing the carton of orange juice and two glasses. "I'll join you."

"Frankie feeling okay?" I ask because she was rubbing her extended belly when we got to their house, yawning, barely able to stay awake.

His eyes light up. "She's good. Just tired. This pregnancy is taking it out of her. She still has three months to go, but Ox is a factor she didn't have the first time. I try to take on more, but he's in a mommy phase. Sometimes she's the only one who can make it better—whatever the fuck was wrong in the first place."

He hands me a glass of OJ. We sit in the living room in silence. He doesn't even turn on the TV to give us something to focus on.

"Listen. Tonight sucked. What you and Taylor have gone through sucks. Rowdy was being a big brother, protecting his sister. The sister she was at fifteen. It's old pain—for y'all—for him. He'll come around."

I try not to flinch at the reminder of her age. Technically, based on where our birthdays fall, I'm barely a year older. But still, it sounds like I robbed the cradle. "And if he doesn't?" There's a chance our friendship can't come back from me knocking up his underage sister.

Jesus. She was pregnant. A wave of nausea rolls through me. How horribly alone did she feel? Was her family there for her at all? Her friends?

"He will." He's so sure.

Moments later, the front door opens. Cap walks in with purpose. Behind him, a leery Rowdy follows at a more reticent pace.

I'm on my feet in an instant, ready to defend myself this time.

Cap holds his hands up. "No. There won't be any fighting. We're here to talk. That's all. Right?" He looks to Rowdy.

"Yeah. I didn't come to fight. I swear, Landry."

Cap pulls me into a surprising hug. It's tight and fierce, and I have a feeling he won't let up until I hug him back. So, I do.

It's been a long time since I've been hugged like this. Maybe never.

"I'm sorry, son." He grips the back of my neck. "I had no idea all the stuff you two have been carrying around. I know you need to work it out with her, but I want to assure you, you're my family too no matter what happens."

A tightness I didn't know I was holding unwinds. I was worried, but just to confirm: "So, I'm not kicked off the team?"

He pulls back, squeezing my shoulders. "Nah, you're stuck with us."

Rowdy moves closer, but so does Gabriel. Rowdy sighs, his head hanging low. "I'm not going to hurt him, okay?"

He can try. I bite my tongue. It's obvious he's all out of fight. "It's alright," I assure Gabriel, honored to be blessed with these guys who come out to protect and fight for you or with you depending on the situation. Before Cap found me, I was a loner, making friends where I could, but something in me was broken.

Even before Taylor. Probably from when my dad left. Cap and his family of misfits started to mend my broken pieces. I have a career and a family with Cap. Mel gave me a place to call my own, where I'm the boss and have a creative release through my music. I'm in a far better place than I was when I was seventeen. I'm devastated by the news of our baby who will never be, but not defeated. I'm not going to ruin my future over it like I did before. I still have hope. Nothing can kill that.

"Listen—"

"No," I interrupt Rowdy. "Let me get this out, then you can say what you need to."

He tips his chin, motioning me to go ahead.

I step away from them, needing space if I'm going to filet my soul wide open before them. "You know we met on Padre Island. I was seventeen. There with friends. I met Taylor and her friends on the beach in front of our hotel. We all hung out. I liked her right away. It was mutual. She didn't look fifteen. I never suspected. She led me to believe we were the same age. I was gone for her after that first night. We spent all our time together. What felt like weeks was, in reality, only a handful of days. We fell in love. Shared our heart and—"

Rowdy holds up his hand. "I get the picture. I don't need a blow by blow."

"I loved her, Rowdy. With every fiber of my being, I loved her. Thought she was my future. I *wanted* her to be my future—my wife." When emotions rise, I turn away, looking out the windows into the dark night. "We made plans to see each other after spring break. But being the stupid kid I was, I didn't think I needed more than her phone number. I never knew her last name. Then she no-showed our last day together.

"I waited. I called. I worried something bad had happened. I looked for you even though I didn't know what you looked like. I thought deep down I might recognize you as her brother if I saw you. Then, I waited some more. Finally, a maid let me in her room, and I confirmed she was gone."

I turn, facing them. "I left my heart in Padre. When I went home, I was a mess. Drinking. Partying. I blew my classes off. After months of that, it all came to a head when I crashed my car and shattered my right arm. I lost my throwing arm, my college scholarships, and any hope of playing in the NFL—after I'd already lost her."

"Damn," Gabriel grumbles under his breath.

"Six years later on the way to your wedding, my heart comes strolling onto your family's plane like she owns the place. Turns out she did because she's your sister. Now, eight years after I first met her, I find out Cap is her dad too, and she was pregnant with our baby at fifteen." I collapse to the couch, worn the fuck out. If he wants to be pissed at me, I can't stop him, and I don't have the energy to fight him right now.

Rowdy paces for a full minute as we wait in silence.

What is Taylor doing?

How is she doing?

If Cap and Rowdy are here, does that mean she's with Reese or Cher?

"Taylor isn't alone, is she?" I can't help asking. I might be upset with her, but I don't want her isolated and hurting.

"She's with Cher. Security is there," Cap advises.

Rowdy stops locking eyes with me, jaw clenched, hands on his hips. "That right there is why I can't be mad at you. You're a good guy. She hurt you, and yet you're worried about her. You're not a player. I've no doubt you were even nicer at seventeen. I don't believe for a second you used her or got her to do anything she wasn't willing to do. She was a wild child. Strong. Stubborn. A fierce, unstoppable force."

"Yeah, she was." A smile tugs at my lips but falls just as quickly. She's not like that anymore. "What happened to squelch that…before…?"

"My parents. They wrapped her up all nice and tight and squeezed the fight out of her. She managed to get some of her spirit back in the last few years, but then—"

"Beau." Asshole extraordinaire. Dead man walking.

"Yep." He sits on the floor, facing me with his knees up, arms resting on them. "But she started to get a little spark back when you two started dating. I had high hopes for y'all." He taps my foot with his. "I still do."

"I think that ship has sailed." I stand to toss my drink and head home. I need to check on the bar and get up early to train. I've got a fight in a week. My heart might not be in it, but if fighting keeps me going and not drinking myself into a stupor, then that's what I need to do.

"Don't give up on her. She made the mistake of not clearing the air before you started dating." Rowdy taps his chest. "I made the situation explosive by being a protective brother and not your friend."

I stop him. "Your sister comes first over our friendship. You don't need to apologize for wanting to protect her, then and now. But do me favor." I point to my face. "Don't hit me again anytime soon."

"Damn, always the good guy, Lan." He grips my shoulder. "I've got your back on this. Take the time you need, just don't give up on her." He pats my chest. "My money's on you."

"I'll second that," Gabriel adds.

"I'll third that." Cap winks and pulls me into another hug, this one shorter and less emotional.

"I'm heading to the bar. I'll catch y'all at the gym mid-morning." For the first time since all of this began approximately two years ago, I feel lighter. There are no more secrets, at least not on my end. I'm not sure how many more secrets Taylor is keeping from me. Will she volunteer the truth or make me work for it?

As I leave, I clock the security guard walking the perimeter. For a moment I'd forgotten some asshole is still out there, threatening my Heartbreaker.

I know who I'll be picturing as I hit the bag tomorrow. As for tonight, I keep an eye out as I drive to the bar, wondering if he's watching. Did he enjoy the show tonight? Is he sitting waiting for Taylor to leave Cap's, or is he following me? I hope it's me. I've a renewed reason to fight, and legal or not, I want to knock his lights out. Permanently.

He took more than my girl's body. He tried to take her fire.

CHAPTER 32

JESS HUGS ME THE SECOND I WALK IN THE BACK OF
Sugarplums. "Taytay, I didn't expect to see you this morning. That's
some heavy shit. I'm really sorry."

I blanch. "Does everyone know?"

"Nah, I was there behind Gabriel and Rowdy with Walker. We heard
that crazy waitress start screaming and came to haul her ass off if need
be. I was at the back door when y'all took it to nature. I sent Reese and
Frankie out to try to calm Rowdy. Didn't really see what happened from
there. Figured Gabriel and the girls could handle it."

I don't remember Reese and Frankie coming out, only Reese getting
in Rowdy's car. But then I wasn't in the clearest state of mind.

Understanding I don't really want to talk, he puts me to work on
making cinnamon rolls. The one task I've nearly perfected.

My mind keeps wandering to Landry. Is he doing okay? Is he alone?
Where did he sleep last night? I nearly burst into tears this morning at
the sight of his clothes in my closet and his shoes on the floor. The emp-
tiness inside seemed to grow tenfold.

I've no idea how I'm going to make it through the day, much less tonight, working at Mel's. I'll take it one second at a time, one hour, one breath until my head hits the pillow, and I do it all over again tomorrow.

And the next.

And the next.

Eventually, it has to not hurt so bad, right?

Eventually?

My face looks like I hit the rear end of a dump truck. I have a purple heart on my face: two round purple-red bruised circles around my eyes melting into a point at my nose with a swollen top lip. It's a sad look and matches my bruised insides. There's no sparring for a couple of days.

Gabriel and Rowdy bust a gut when they spot me sauntering in. *Assholes.*

"Man, I'm so sorry." Rowdy laughs, bending over.

"Yeah, I can tell." There's no heat in my words. I was the idiot not wearing headgear. I've got an appointment later with some leeches to remove the bruising. I can't go into my fight looking like I just had one. It won't heal the broken nose, but the leeches release a protein that reduces clotting and promotes healing. I figure it can't hurt.

I leave the assholes to their snickering and meet Jonah at the speedbag. He silently tapes my hands, only raising his eyes to mine occasionally.

"You want to talk about it?" Jonah is our quiet Zen master, shrink, big brother, nursemaid, and babysitter. The latter I'm not sure he cares for.

"No, do you?"

He chuckles under his breath. "Time. You both need time."

I feel like we've had more than enough of that. Nearly a decade wasted. Secretly wanting who I thought I'd never see again while believing I got exactly what I deserved—a whole bunch of nothing.

Ignoring my self-pity and pretending like my upcoming fight is my only care in the world, I picture Beau's face and take it out on the speedbag.

I waited until the last minute to leave my apartment above the bar, which feels entirely desolate without Taylor in it, though she truly never was, other than the quick visit the night of the cookout when I found out Cap is her father too. Now that I know what it's like to share a space with her, I doubt I'll feel comfortable in any room she's not in.

Descending the stairs two at a time, I take my sad ass to the bar, nodding when greeted by employees and eager patrons ready to get their drink on. It's Tuesday, and I'm grateful it's not a live music night, though I'm sure I could fill the bar on a regular basis if every night was a live night. Business is good the way it is. Maybe after this shit with Taylor and her stalker are resolved, I'll consider changing the line-up. I'd need more employees to cover the additional work on top of the second manager I need to hire.

I'll let tomorrow's Landry worry about that. Today's Landry can't stop staring at the Heartbreaker across the room with a plastered smile on her face. As she turns, her eyes lift to mine and stop. She freezes for a split second, and in that second, her smile turns genuine. Her eyes beckon to my soul to take her in my arms and heal the void between us. Then, just as fast, the moment is broken when someone walks between us. She blinks, dips her head and hurries off to put in her order.

That's the last time I feel her eyes on me all night.

I move to check on Jake and see if he needs anything restocked. It's a mindless job I can do in my sleep. I don't make it far before Ruby slides into my path in full pout mode.

"Hey, boss man."

"Ruby." The chill in my tone can in no way be misconstrued as warmth. But watch her try.

She twirls her hair, eyeing me from under her lashes. "I'm sorry about my crazy yesterday." She lifts a hand to touch me.

I snag it in mid-air. "Don't."

"What? I just—"

"Whatever lie you're about to spout, save it. I'm not interested in apologies or excuses. The only reason you still have your job is because I know you need it to help support your family. You keep a wide berth around Taylor. Don't even think of giving her a hard time. One step out of line and you're fired. Understood?"

I wait long enough to hear her acquiesce, then sidestep her like shit on the sidewalk.

I've been off since I woke up and remembered my life is a total shit show, at least where Landry is concerned. It took me most of the morning at the bakery to feel nearly normal. Then, right before leaving, as I refilled the display cases out front, I thought I caught a glimpse of Beau. It was just out of the corner of my eye and only a second or two of him looking through the store windows. By the time I gave the figure my full attention, he was gone.

My *feeling off* status returned full force and hasn't let up since. Seeing Ruby talking to Landry doesn't help any. But he didn't let her touch him, and if his icy demeanor is any indication of how he feels about her, she should need a sweater right about now.

"Hey, beautiful," Jake greets me at the bar. "Whatcha need?"

"Three drafts and a Corona hold the lime."

"Coming up."

Brady raps his knuckles on the bar, offering a scary smile at a woman at the end of the bar, but his words are for me, "You doing okay? Any more sightings to report?"

"Nope. I'm good." I glance at the woman. "You look like a crazed killer. Stop with the fake smile."

He scowls, silently saying *what fake smile?*

"There. That's believable. Besides, women like the grumpy, big guys."

"I'm not picking up a woman," he grumbles.

"Not with that smile you're not." I load the drinks on my tray as Jake slides them over. "Where's Ramona tonight?"

"She had a thing."

"Ah, hate when that happens." I wink and slip into the crowd delivering my order.

Rick, the other security guy, acting as a runner, nods as he passes. That's about the extent of our interactions. He does his thing, and I do mine, and if all goes okay, we don't need to talk more than that. It's calming in its simplicity. He's not here to make friends. I've got bigger fish to fry. We work.

As the night trudges on, my energy wanes, and my happy façade slips. I just want to be home, lying on my bed in pjs and eating salted caramel ice cream from the gallon tub as I watch a movie or binge a new series on one of my many streaming services.

Instead, I pull myself up, paste on a smile and serve these people with a shine I don't feel, and a tight grip on my emotions that could explode on them at any moment.

I'm a walking IED (Imminent Emotional Devastation). Beware.

CHAPTER 33

I T'S FIGHT NIGHT IN VEGAS, AND MY EX IS ONE OF the star attractions. All the Black Ops guys have gone to cheer Landry on, including Cam and Cap. It seems like half our usual patrons have gone, as Mel's is dead for a Saturday. The place was abuzz about his upcoming fight for the four days or so leading up to it.

I tried to ignore it.

I try not take it personally that no one invited me to go.

I try to not look the direction of his office or the bar where he'd usually be if he were here. Which he's not.

Because his big fight is tonight.

And I'm here with the undesirables who didn't get *asked* to go or didn't *want* to go.

I sit wholeheartedly on the first spectrum of the *didn't get asked*. I *wanted* to go. I would have if I wasn't such a pouty baby about not going where I'm clearly not wanted.

Am I the pariah? The outcast? The ex everyone wishes would disappear?

"Don't look, but Ruby's been eyeing you since we opened." Ramona exchanges her full tray for my empty one.

"She's probably hoping I'll break down in tears, missing Landry." I don't even care to look in Ruby's direction. She hasn't said a word to me since the incident where my worst secret was revealed. She could drop dead, and I'm pretty sure I'd just step right over her body like she didn't exist. I point to my now full tray. "What are these?"

"Table ten. I needed an excuse to talk to you."

"Yeah, cause *hi* just wouldn't have been believable." I roll my eyes and deliver the drinks to *her* table.

"Well, are you?" Ramona tags along as I enter a food order I was on my way to do before she sidetracked me with her table's drinks.

"Am I what?"

"Going to break down for missing him?"

I blink at her for a second before returning my gaze to the computer screen. "Not if I can help it." I leave her to do her security job slash pretend to be a server thing.

If I'm going to cry, it certainly won't be in front of Ruby.

This guy's a giant. He didn't look this big in the pictures or videos I scoped out the last few weeks. I was in my head during the weigh-in this morning. I don't remember laying an eye on him until he stepped into the octagon.

But then my eyes have only seen Beau on every stranger's face. I lash out, toppling my opponent with a roundhouse kick. I'm going with the *bigger they are, the harder they fall* mentality. I nearly get him locked in a Kimura hold, but he twists out at the last second using the side of the cage as leverage.

I should have gone for the Omoplata version using my legs instead. Next time.

I bounce to my feet, giving him just enough space for me to spot any weakness or injury. He cracks his neck and dives at me, going for a body slam. I pivot at the last second and deliver high kick to the face as he passes, falling to the mat.

This guy can't stay on his feet. The bigger they are…

The bell rings.

I take to my corner, sweeping the seats where my guys sit. Disappointment lingers as I ask Jonah what I already know, "Did she come?"

All I get is a quick head shake from Jonah as Coach talks in my ear, "Quit playing. Knock—"

I'm on my feet, ready to go before the bell even rings to start the next round. I don't have time for words. I need action.

"Taylor?" Ruby motions toward the hall I've glanced down too many times, hoping to see Landry, regardless of knowing he's not here.

"I'll be right back," I tell Leo as he fills my drink order. I should ignore her, but I'm curious. Is she going to gloat, knowing Landry and I are on the outs? Our falling out doesn't have anything to do with her, but I'm sure she'll be happy to take the credit. I stop in front of her, popping a hip. I'd file my nails and pop some gum if I had either or thought it could help me appear any less interested. "Yeah?"

"Can we—" She motions down the hall. "It'll just take a sec."

"What…" I follow because, despite everything, I don't want to be rude, but… "Make it quick. Jake is filling my order."

"Yep." She pushes the back door open, stepping aside enough for me to slip out.

I turn to face her. "Okay. What?"

"It's just—"

An arm bands my waist, and there's a sharp pinch in my neck.

"Ruby!"

She only smiles and slips inside, the door shutting behind her as I struggle against the body holding me. "Help!" I try to scream, but he covers my mouth as I'm dragged away from the door.

"Settle, James."

No. No. I blink as my vision skews and my body refuses to work. Then… darkness.

The asshole hits my cheek right beside my nose that's barely started to heal. It stings like a motherfu… I blink to clear the tears, raging with punch after punch: right, right, left, right, left, right, right, left to his face and upper body. All while fending off his strikes that are barely a blip on my pain threshold. His lip and left eye are bleeding. I hit him with an uppercut seconds before the bell sounds.

In my corner, I plop into the stool. Let Jonah do his thing and catch sight of Cap in my periphery, giving Coach the stink-eye.

I spit out my mouthguard. "What's going on?"

"Nothing," Coach assures. "You ready to end this?"

"Hell yeah." More than he knows. My face should be killing me, but the adrenaline pumping through my body has me buzzing. I've got a whole other fight left in me.

Ding

"Bring it." I jump to my feet, thumping my chest, growling at the asshole as he leaves his corner thinking he can best me.

I don't think so. I need to end this.

I charge, hitting him with a flying superman punch square on the chin. His head jars back.

I follow him to the mat with the roar of the arena near deafening. One-two punch. Left. Right.

He goes slack.

The ref falls between us, forcing me out, keeping me from landing another punch.

Bell sounds.

It's done.

The crowd is on their feet.

I'm announced the winner.

I raise my arms in victory, circling, looking for my team, wanting them to share in my win, confirming I deserve their faith and commitment in me.

But what I find is the solemn faces of Coach, Rowdy, and Jonah that try to perk up when I lock on them. Frowning, I spot Cap and Gabriel heading up the aisle, away from my win.

What. The. Fuck?

When I finally get out of the cage, Jonah is there.

"Tell me," I huff, trying to calm down, dripping with sweat and the need to find Taylor coursing through my blood. My win falls flat without her here to celebrate with me.

"Taylor is missing," Jonah advises, worry riddling his demeanor.

"Missing?"

"Come on." Rowdy pulls me toward the exit in a run.

"What happened?"

"We don't know much. Cap is talking to Detective Bryant. The police are on their way to Mel's. Taylor followed Ruby down the hall, and that's the last anyone saw her. Ruby is being held in your office awaiting the cops." Rowdy's phone rings. He charges the exit, answering in a full run.

I realize I don't have my phone, clothes or anything. But I follow. I'll run all the way to Mel's or to wherever Taylor is if need be.

Please be okay, I chant on repeat as we leap into Cap's truck and tear out of the area parking lot.

Where the fuck was her security?

CHAPTER 34

MY HEAD POUNDS. I SQUINT THROUGH BLINDING
light, groaning as I turn my head and a wave of nausea rolls through
me. "I'm going to be sick." My words come out slurred. My tongue
is too big for my mouth and dry like I've been sucking on cotton balls.

"There's a bucket on the floor next to your head if you're going to
throw up."

No.

I turn toward the voice I'd hoped to never hear again, only my vision
is too blurry to make out his face. Not that I could ever forget the sharp
angles of his chiseled features, floppy black hair, and piercing black eyes.
I'd thought him handsome at one point, before he...

I heave, managing to roll enough to puke into the awaiting pail. *He
planned this,* my mind screams as I continue to empty my stomach, gag-
ging and huffing for air.

There's nothing left to heave, and yet...

After what feels like an eternity, I slump against the seat, sucking in
oxygen, closing my eyes.

If I die now, this is as bad as it gets.

No! I can't die. Not like this. Not with puke on my face and barely having put up a fight.

We've stopped. A door opens and closes, then a moment later, the door closest to my head opens. Fresh air rushes in.

"Here, James, let me clean you up." Something cool swipes across my mouth and face. "Drink." He forces my mouth open and pours cool liquid inside.

Water.

I reflexively swallow before I remember what he did to me before. He drugged me in something I drank—or I believe that's how he drugged me. Either way, I can't drink any more.

But I didn't drink anything earlier at the bar, nothing that he could have gotten to. "Did you shoot something into my neck?" I still remember the pinch.

"Ketamine. Just a small dose. Didn't knock you out very long, but long enough to get on the road. It does have some nasty side effects though. I'll empty the bucket and be right back."

As soon as the door shuts, I look around, then peek out the window. He's only a few feet away dumping the bucket in the grass on the side of a highway, pulled over like any other person might when you have a sick passenger. I try to sit up but barely make it a few inches before the nausea hits again, my vision spinning. I lie back down before I pass out.

The door opens. The bucket is placed on the floor by my head. "Here. I brought you this." He slides a white pillow under my head.

I fight the sigh that tries to escape at the soft coolness against my face.

Then it hits me: he brought a pillow? My stomach rolls again, knowing he planned this in detail. Did Ruby know? Or did she just think he was some guy who had a crush on me? Does she hate me enough to be an accomplice to Beau's madness and put me in real danger? Is she that stupid? That spiteful?

"You're shaking. Do you want a blanket?"

"No. Hot."

"Another side effect." He kisses my forehead, muttering, "Sleep," and shuts the door.

I want to wipe his kiss from my skin, but I can hardly move. My whole body hurts from shaking so hard, and my head is pounding like a jackhammer. I may not know where we are or where we're going, but I do know we're in my car.

I hope he's not smart enough to know how to disengage the theft tracker on it. I also hope Cap, Rowdy, Landry, or the police realize it's a way to find me before... before it's too late.

I fought sleep for as long as I could. Figuring I'd need the rest, I let my body fall, hoping it would aid in getting the drugs out of my system. When I wake to the car slowing, I keep my eyes closed. It's best if he thinks I'm still asleep, affected by the bottled water he placed in my hands after forcing the first few sips down my throat.

I vaguely remember dropping a bottled water in the back seat a few days ago. I meant to grab it when I pulled into Cap's garage but forgot. I don't remember seeing it when I was getting sick. Maybe it's under one of the seats.

Beau turns left and then right, slowing to a stop. There's a long pause before the engine turns off. I keep my eyes softly closed, trying to relax and not think about him staring at me from the front seat, his mind racing with all he wants to do to me.

I'm asleep. He needs to think I'm sleeping.

With a soft sigh, his door opens, shuts. The locks engage. He's not planning on opening my door, or he wouldn't have locked it. I squint a peek, looking around without turning my head. When I don't see him, I open further and lift up, making it till I can see out the driver's side window, catching sight of him walking into the gas station.

In a flash, I sit up, ignoring my body's protests, and lean across the middle console, keeping my head low to swap my water bottle for his. He's only taken a few sips, so it's about as full as mine. I'm praying he won't notice.

I feel under the seats for the bottled water I hope is still here and snag it on my second attempt. Quickly, I open it and take a few deep drinks. I dump half of his water in the bucket so it looks like I've drank more and therefore am more drugged. I finish my water, thankful my stomach doesn't reject it, and tuck the empty bottle back under the seat.

In my movements I catch sight of my left foot, chained to the door handle with about three feet of slack. I test the back door. It won't open. He has the childproof lock engaged. I should have considered running the second he entered the station, but drugging him seemed the more foolproof option. Now that I can't get more than three feet away, I don't regret that choice. The gas station is desolate. Probably the only other person here is the person working the cash register. Would they help me if I screamed?

Would Beau hurt them to keep me silent?

Landry's face pops in my head. My heart races for a whole other reason.

Will I ever see him again?

Will I get a chance to make things right?

Do I deserve that chance?

All those questions ping in my head as I choose to lie down, pretending I'm in a drug haze. If he tries to touch me again, I will fight him tooth and nail. I won't be so easily subdued this time.

This time I'm prepared to fight.

If he thinks he's getting a repeat, he's sorely mistaken.

CHAPTER 35

CLOSED DOWN MEL'S, SENT EVERYONE HOME. THE police moved Ruby to the police station. Good riddance.

The FBI are called in as a favor to the DA. Mel's is serving as a ground zero and headquarters in the search for my Songbird.

Hours of uncertainty pass. Anger and regret ride the wave of adrenaline from my fight. I need my girl. I need to know she's alright. I need to make it right—make *us* right.

While we wait, Rowdy forces me into the shower, probably the fastest of my life. One of the guys dropped off my stuff from the fight. I throw on jeans and a t-shirt and pocket my phone, but check it first just to see if I have a message or missed call from Taylor. My heart drops when I see I've nothing.

Please, God keep her safe.

Not even thirty minutes later, Cap, Rowdy, and I board a private plane arranged by the DA. We know the general direction we're heading, but we're not sure where we'll end up landing. The FBI have officially taken over the case, given that Beau has taken Taylor across state lines, making it a federal offense, and into Arizona, according to her car's LoJack.

I've never been so relieved to find out Beau isn't smart enough to ditch her car. Or maybe it's arrogance. He got away with it the first time. He figures he's on a roll.

Two guys simply introduced as Web and Tumble Weed join us minutes before departure. The two of them and Cap huddle in the back with a handful of FBI agents.

"Who are they?" I ask Rowdy, referring to Web and Tumble Weed.

"Marine buddies. The DA and those two served under Cap. From what Gabriel has shared, their connection is tight and unbreakable. Web is CIA. Tumble Weed was a state pen warden. I'm not sure what he's doing now."

I'm thankful Cap has some wide-reaching connections. I don't believe for a second it's normal for the family of the victim to be included in the manhunt. Once again, I'm in awe of the incredible family Cap has amassed, by blood or choice.

Cap's gaze meets mine the second he looks our way. He says something to the guys surrounding him and stands. By the look on his face, I know a decision has been made, and he has news.

I just pray it's better than the dark thoughts running rampant in my head.

A warm hand caresses up my neck to my jaw and back down, pausing over my breasts with a firm squeeze. *Landry*. My sleepy thoughts race to him. He found me, and I'm safe in his bed.

I sigh.

"Wake up, James," Beau's rasp slams me into reality.

I'm not saved.

I'm caught in Beau's noose, and I'm hoping I don't hang.

I roll toward the back of the seat, wrapping my arms around myself, murmuring, "Sleepy," hoping he'll think I'm too drugged up to understand what's happening.

That's how I felt last time, with only blips of horrifying clarity that soon faded into nothingness. For some reason he hasn't started while I've been unconscious this time.

"Too tired, beautiful?" He plants a kiss on my cheek. "We have time. I was hoping for a taste, and I'd prefer you were lucid this time. I haven't been able to stop thinking about you. I want to hear how much you love my touch. How you've missed me and love me. It'll be better this time; now that you know my touch, we can really focus on what *I* like." He groans, squeezing my ass, lamenting, "I've missed you, James."

I want to barf. I want to rail at him. Tell him every vile thing I think of him.

But I don't.

I remain still, feigning sleep.

Praying, praying, praying they find me before it's too late.

"What do you mean they've stopped?" I pace away from Cap as far as the plane allows and turn. "Is he—" I flash to Rowdy's impassive face and back to Cap, who wears nearly the exact same expression.

"We don't know, son. We've flown past them. We're going to land in Flagstaff and take cars from there. You and Rowdy will stay with the plane."

"No." Rowdy stands. "We're going."

Cap shakes his head, determined. "No. This is official FBI business. I'm only going because of my service experience and rank—and my con- nections. They won't allow civilians to tag along. You're only here because this is not their plane. *They* tagged along with us. But from here, it's by the books."

One of the FBI calls Cap over. They talk for a moment before Cap returns. "They're on the move again." He flashes to me. "That's a good thing. Moving, he can't hurt her." He pats the back of my seat. "Buckle up. We'll be landing soon."

I do as directed as Cap takes his seat in the rear of the plane, but it's infuriating to be a trained fighter told to sit down while the grownups handle the problem. "I feel like a kid who just got told by his dad it's an adults-only party."

"I think that's exactly what just happened."

"I love her," I admit as I'm not sure he fully comprehends the depth of my feelings even after all of these years and why it's hard to do nothing.

"I know you do, Lan. She's going to be fine. She's a fighter," he assures me.

How in the hell can you know that?

"And if he hurts her again?" I concentrate out the window, not able to stand the pain flashing in his eyes that rivals my own.

"Then we'll kill him. And *still*, Taylor will be fine because she's a fighter."

Fight, baby. Fight for you. Fight for us. Never stop fighting.

I must have dozed off again. I come to and nearly roll off the seat as the car swerves one direction and quickly swerves the other. I sit up as Beau's head bobs down and then jerks back up. We're on a long patch of highway. It's pitch black out.

Another swerve has me flying to the left door where my foot is chained. I grab the seatbelt, but before I can put it on, I reach forward, between the driver's seat and the middle console, and press the button to release his belt. I quickly latch mine, then grab the pillow I've been sleeping on and place it in my lap. I'm not sure what good it'll do, but it might help. It can't hurt.

Beau mumbles something and takes a long drink of water, throwing the empty bottle to the passenger's seat.

He finished it all.

I'm elated and terrified.

He must have kept drinking, thinking it would keep him awake. It's having the opposite effect. His movements are jerky and extreme. He's going to kill us if he doesn't slow down.

"Stop!" I yell, hoping he'll hit the brakes before he passes out behind the wheel.

He does slam on the brakes, but he jerks the wheel to the left at the same time.

I hold my breath and place my head in the pillow in my lap, gripping the bottom of the seat seconds before we flip.

Weightless, hanging in midair, I try to scream but make no sound, or I am and I just can't hear it. It's the strangest sensation, like the drop of a rollercoaster.

But we aren't weightless, and gravity has a toll.

The impact is substantial when car meets road again, and again, and again. Flipping, flipping, and flipping.

I'm going to die.

I'm going to die.

I'm going to die.

CHAPTER 36

"**A**RE WE REALLY GOING TO SIT HERE AND WAIT?" I watch as the taillights from the awaiting cars speed off the tarmac and into the night.

"No. Just give them a few more minutes." Rowdy looks about as calm as I feel, which is absolutely not calm at all.

My phone pings with a text. Checking it, I break into a smile. My agitation eases a tad. "Come on." I head for the open door and charge down the steps, only hitting them once before I land on the pavement. Rowdy's footfall follows.

"I wondered how long you'd sit there before deciding to take matters into your own hands," Det. Bryant muses, standing behind the open driver's door. "Get in."

You don't have to tell us twice. I hop in the front with Rowdy in the back, leaning over the front seats, asking, "How'd you know?"

"Cap texted me. He didn't believe you boys would stay behind. He asked if I'd keep an eye on you."

Alarm bells go off. "You're not taking us to Taylor?"

He flashes me a smile. "Yeah, of course, I am. We'll just be a few minutes behind them. Cap didn't want ya'll in the mix of whatever goes down. But he didn't want to leave you out either."

"Are you allowed to do this?" Rowdy asks.

"It was my case first. I'm just following up. Making myself available in case they have any questions."

Thank God. I study his phone clipped to a holder on the dash, a map leading us to a moving dot. "Is that them?"

"Yeah, I'm tracking Cap's phone."

"Gotta love the man." Rowdy sits back, arms spread wide.

Flashing lights ahead have me sitting up, straining to see what all the commotion's about.

Det. Bryant's phone rings. Cap's name flashes on the screen. The detective answers it on the car's speakers. "Cap."

"Get here now."

"We see the flashing lights. What happened?"

"Here. Now." Cap disconnects.

"Fuck," leaves all three of our mouths as the detective speeds up.

"Cap?" Is he really here? Am I hallucinating?

"I'm here, Taylor. Don't move. Let the firemen work to get you free."

"My head—"

"I know, honey. Be strong. Hold on."

The worry on his face has tears burning my eyes. I look at the nice fireman taking my vitals as someone else works near my feet. "I'm stuck."

"Yes, ma'am, you are. But not for long."

I feel weird. "Am I dying?"

"Not if we have any say in the matter. And we're pretty determined to get you out of the car alive and fighting."

That's nice. He's a nice fireman.

"Cap, where's Beau?" I can't really tell, but it looks like the front seat is empty.

"You don't need to worry about him." His voice sounds strange.

A beeping noise distracts me. I'm lightheaded, floaty. "I wish Landry were here."

"He's on his way. Hold on, Taylor. Fight," Cap insists.

"Her vitals are dropping. We need to get her out now," the nice fireman beside me advises. His reassuring smile doesn't mask the worry in his eyes.

"Almost there," a muffled voice comes from below. *What's he doing down there?*

"Cap?"

"Yeah, honey."

"I can't see." My voice trembles, fades, falls.

"She's coding!"

"Let me through!" I shove a police officer and barrel forward, his threats falling at my feet.

Cap turns, his face pale and his eyes glassy.

"No." I stop cold.

"Landry," he grouses.

"No." I back away. *No, please, God. No.*

Rowdy skids to a halt beside me. "Dad?"

"Stay there." He holds up his hand, his gaze flashing over his shoulder to the car.

"Cap?" I barely get his name out as I fight to draw enough air.

Don't say it.

Don't say it.

Don't stay it.

Please, God, don't take her from me—from us.

"Give em a minute," Cap's voice cracks.

Rowdy grabs my arm. "Don't lose faith."

I point at the car—*her* car. "Nobody can survive that." Every inch of her Maserati SUV is smashed; the roof is caved in, more in the front than the back, but barely any room for a head—

"Landry." Cap steps closer then pauses.

I shake my head, avert my eyes.

She's gone.

I've lost her. I've lost her this time for good.

"Landry," he tries again.

"Please don't." I can't take it. I can't stand to hear the words.

"You need to ride with her." Rowdy or Cap are pulling me forward.

I can't see through my tears. "I can't."

"You can, son." Cap squeezes my shoulder, moving me forward, pushing me up into the ambulance.

Why is he doing this?

I flop onto a bench seat in the ambulance.

"Be strong," Cap's words float through the air as the doors close.

I double over, closing my eyes. Ignoring the gurney and the lifeless body on it. "I loved you," I sob into my hands and the black abyss of my life without her. "I *love* you. I love you. Forever I will love you."

"Does that mean you forgive me?" a scratchy but familiar voice asks.

My mind is playing tricks. Why would the paramedic say that?

197

"What did you say?" I rub at my face, blinking, staring into the face of a woman I don't know.

The paramedic points down to the gurney. My eyes track the trajectory of her finger.

Down.

Down.

Down.

Beautiful green eyes smile back at me. "Hi."

"Taylor?"

"Are you expecting someone else?" She tries to smile but winces. Her face is swollen and bruised, looking about like I did after her brother broke my nose.

"Songbird." I reach for her hand but hesitate. I don't want to hurt her.

She takes my hand with surprising strength. "Dually."

I'd fall to my knees if there was room. My forehead hits our joined hands, and my shoulders shake as sobs of relief rack my body.

"Hey. Hey." Her hand tugs from mine and brushes my face. "You didn't answer me. Am I forgiven?"

I sob harder, nodding. "Always. Am I?" I beseech her with my eyes, palming her face as gently as I can.

"You've done nothing wrong," she insists.

"I let you believe my anger was more important than our love." I kiss her hand, closing my eyes, saying a silent prayer. *Thank you, God, for keeping her safe.* "It's not." I lock on her horribly abused but absolutely lovely face. "Nothing is more important than us. I love you, Songbird."

Tears fall from the corner of her eyes. "Promise you'll tell me every day?"

"More. I promise."

She nods as best she can in the neck brace. "I love you, Landry. I never stopped. I never will."

"Then marry me. Put me out of my misery. Let me show you every day how much I love you." It's a shit proposal, but if I've learned anything, time is a precious commodity, nearly as precious as her.

Her smile has her busted lower lip bleeding, but damn if she's still not the most beautiful sight I've ever had the pleasure of beholding.

"Please, baby. I don't want to waste another minute being away from you." I palm the side of her face, bending closer. "I love you, Taylor. Marry me today, tomorrow, as soon as we can. Just say *yes*."

"You won't regret it? I'm sorry about the baby and not telling you sooner. I didn't want to give you one more reason to hate me."

"I never hated you. I was angry, hurt, but never hate. Never you." I kiss her hand. "None of it matters compared to the love we share. Say you'll be mine. Forever."

"Forever," she whispers.

"Is that a *yes*?" I need *the* words.

"Yes, I'll marry you." She brings our joined hands to her mouth, touching mine tenderly. "You're the only man I'd ever want to marry, Dually."

"You were always mine," my scratchy voice cracks as I swipe at her tears. I nearly lost her.

"I was. Same for you." She catches a tear on my cheek. "I want to sing with you forever."

"I think we can make that work." I'll do anything to make my Heartbreaker happy, not that singing with her is a hardship. Doing *anything* with her is an honor. "I'm not joking about marrying you today."

She laughs then groans. "You better call Cap, see if he can pull some strings. I might be staying a night or two in the hospital."

"I'll be right there beside you, Songbird."

"I wouldn't want you anywhere else."

THE END

Can't get enough? Want to know what's next for Landry and Taylor? Keep reading for their Epilogue and a chance to get exclusive BONUS Scenes for newsletter subscribers.
dl.bookfunnel.com/71ggnkfcfz

Jess' story is next in MUSTANG. Add it to your TBR.
https://smarturl.it/MUSTANG_TBR

In the meantime, if you picked up COWBOY without reading the other books in the series, check out all the yummy alphas in my *Black Ops MMA* Series. They're tough, determined, and sometimes too alpha for their own good. **NO MERCY** is Book 1 in the series. Gabriel "No Mercy" Stone fell hard for his best friend's woman. To hide his feelings, he ignored her and treated her like dirt. But when things go south with her boyfriend, Gabriel is there to pick up the pieces. *When it comes to protecting his Angel, he has no mercy.*
https://smarturl.it/BlackOpsMMA_Amz

Are best friend's sister, friends to lovers, or second chance romances more your style? Then check out my . Book 1, , is a heart-wrenching romance about a millionaire in the making and his best friend's younger sister. Joseph is everything Samantha is afraid to want, yet she's never wanted to be noticed so badly in her life. Samantha shouldn't even be on Joseph's radar, and yet she is from the day she walks in the room, making him want what's not his to take.
https://smarturl.it/UYSeries_Amz

Are First Responders your jam? Then check out charity anthology benefitting Grassroots Wildland Firefighters organization.
My contribution is **Wildflower.**
What happens when a firefighter has a crush on the shy, free-spirited flower shop owner?
Click here to find out!
Books2read.com/HeroeswHHV2

Want romance with an otherworldly connection? Then check out Theo and Lauren's epic romance in . When Life put them together, the Universe noticed. What they didn't know is that they were made for each other. Literally.
https://smarturl.it/TRTR_Amz

This is a dream for me to be able to share my love of writing with you. If you liked this book, please consider leaving a review on Amazon and/or on Goodreads.

Personal recommendations to your friends and loved ones is
a great compliment too.
Please share, follow, join my newsletter, and help spread the word—let everyone know how much you love Landry and Taylor.
dmckdavis.com/subscribe

EPILOGUE ONE

HOURS LATER

SHE'S BEEN IN SURGERY FOR HOURS. *HOURS.* I DON'T think any of us have taken a seat. We're pacing the Flagstaff Memorial Hospital ER, wearing out the floor and the patience of the staff. "Please, gentlemen, take a seat. The doctor will be out shortly with news."

Yeah, I nod and keep walking. If I stop, I might fall, and if I fall, I might not get back up. And that won't do. I have to be strong for my girl.

Please, God, let her be okay.

She was lucid in the ambulance, agreed to marry me, for fuck's sake. Then she started having trouble breathing.

Once we arrived at the ER, they rushed her away. When she was stable, they ran tests and took her into surgery for a collapsed lung and her injured left leg. I haven't seen her since.

Beau, the asshole, had her chained to the damn door. *Chained.*

I'd kill the dead-man-walking if he wasn't already dead. Cap informed me of that welcomed news after he arrived with Rowdy, Det. Bryant, and his Marine pals. Beau was flung from the car about a hundred and fifty feet from where the car came to rest.

I'm thankful for his death for so many reasons, one of which being I won't chance going to prison for taking his life. But mainly for Taylor's peace of mind in knowing he can never harm her again.

My girl.

My Heartbreaker.

My Songbird.

She survived.

She's a fighter, and she's going to be my wife.

I find Cap and grip his arms. "I'm going to marry her." I catch his frazzled gaze.

"What?"

"I'm going to marry Taylor."

He pats my arm. "That's great, son. I think you should. When she's on her feet, we'll start planning."

"No." I shake my head. "As soon as she wakes up. I'll get the hospital chaplain to marry us. She said *yes.*" The best news of the day after her surviving.

"Lan," Rowdy starts, but I stop him.

"We've wasted too much time as it is. We're not waiting another minute, day, week, month, or year more than we have to. Whatever happens. Whether she recovers fully or not. We belong together. She's my other half. You get that, don't you?"

Cap and Rowdy share a look and clamp onto my shoulders. "Yeah, we get that."

"Let me see what I can do to help." Cap steps away to talk to his Marine friends.

"Taylor dreamt of a big wedding," Rowdy offers as we stand, staring at the double doors, waiting for news.

"She can still have the big wedding." I catch his gaze. "*This* one will be for us." I never want to dismiss her dreams or be the reason they don't come to fruition. She didn't mention a big wedding, but then we weren't in a big-wedding kind of discussion. If that's what my girl wants, that's what she'll get the moment she's able to throw the wedding of her dreams.

Opening my eyes to find Landry staring down at me floods me with relief. Despite the pain encompassing my whole body, only one thing seems important.

Was it real?

"Did I dream you proposed to me?" I cough, my throat sore and scratchy, my voice barely working.

"Here." He's quick to grab a Styrofoam cup, holding the straw to my mouth. Worry lines his red-rimmed eyes. I tentatively sip the cool water as he replies, "Yeah, Songbird. You're not backing out on me, are you?"

"Never." I'd marry him this minute if it were possible.

He tentatively touches my face. "I nearly lost you."

His teary eyes do crazy things to my insides. Not that I enjoy seeing him cry, but it stokes the flame deep in my heart knowing he cares. "It was a detour. That's all."

He chuckles, nodding. "Hmm." He kisses my forehead. "No more detours. You scared the shit out of me. I thought..." his voice cracks, and closing his eyes, he leans into my neck, hiding.

"I'm here. I've no intention of leaving you again." I grip his shirt, needing to see his face. "When are you going to marry me?"

He laughs and snorts, swiping at his nose. He's a mess, and I love it. "Today. Tomorrow. As soon as you feel up to it."

"Tomorrow is good." I don't have a damn thing to wear, but as long as he's by my side, I could get married in my hospital gown and feel like the prettiest woman alive. But I wouldn't mind a shower first.

"You're going to be more sore tomorrow. So, if you need more time—"

"I don't need more time. I'll do it right now if I can just brush my teeth first."

He laughs again, and it loosens every knot inside me that worried I'd never see the lighter side of him again.

"I thought a lot about this, you know. You and me. Forever." I take another drink. "As hard as the years have been between when we first met and now, I'm not sure I'd change it. I mean, how likely is it we'd still be together?"

"Taylor." He sits on the edge of the bed, leaning down, eye to eye. He's not denying it. Maybe he's wondered the same thing.

"Losing you makes me appreciate having you now more than I ever could without that painful loss." I hate that I hurt him, but I'm less selfish now, learning to appreciate the smaller things in life. I was too self-centered, thought the world revolved around me.

He nods. "No rainbows without a little rain." He kisses my hand. "I've wondered the same. I don't know if I'd go as far as to say I wouldn't change anything, knowing how badly you've been hurt." He tenderly runs his fingers along my jaw. "You could have died tonight." His eyes mist over.

"I didn't. But..." Can I admit it?

"What? It's okay. Say whatever's on your mind."

"I switched the water bottles. I unbuckled his seatbelt. I—"

"You did what you needed to do to survive against someone you know was evil. He had every intention of hurting you, Taylor. Don't forget that. You fought the only way you could—with your brain—and survived."

"He died because of me." I hate the tears that fall. Am I weak for caring about the life of a guy who would have raped me—again—and who knows what else?

"He died because of the plans he set in motion. He shot you up with drugs and followed it with a drugged-water chaser. He chained you. He had nothing but bad intentions." He clenches his jaw, looking out the window for a moment before turning back to me.

"Don't shed a tear for him. He doesn't deserve it. There's one less bad guy on the streets because of you. I doubt you were his first victim. He was too smooth, knew how to get the drugs and how to use them. You saved other women from falling victim to him. You saved *yourself*, and honestly, that's all I care about. You do whatever you have to do to live. Always." His kisses my hand again and stands. "If you feel up to it, Cap and Rowdy would like to see you."

"Love you." It feels good to say that. Freeing. I'm blessed to be here to even be able to see him, much less love him.

He leans down, close enough to kiss, but he doesn't. "You're my world, Songbird. Thank you for fighting. I wouldn't want to live a day without you in it." His presses his lips to my forehead. "Love you."

Cam's tears are nearly as hard to witness as Landry's. "I'm so glad you're okay." He glances at my elevated leg. "Or going to be okay. We'll get you the best care. You'll be good as new. Oh, Dad is flying in. So, yeah, sorry about that."

I'm not. Maybe it's time to make peace. He did raise me, after all. He may not be Cap, but he's a good man in his own way, and he loves me. He loved Mom. He loves Cam, even though Cam isn't ready to forgive, but maybe this trip will change things. "I'm not sorry. It's time to make peace."

He nods and glances at Cap, who's holding up the far wall with Landry, both giving me a moment with my brother. "I'm not sure that's possible."

"I could have died today, Cam. Yet, here I am. I lost my other half when I was fifteen and now I have him back. It seems like almost anything is possible if we want it bad enough."

He harrumphs. "Maybe I don't want it bad enough. Or at all."

I squeeze his hand. "That's your prerogative. But don't be mad if I decide to do otherwise and take a chance on hope. How would you feel if you messed up, and Killian never forgave you?"

"It would kill me. Are you going to read Mom's letter?"

He had to go remind me of that.

"I think I should. It's been long enough. When I get home. Do you regret reading yours?"

"Hell no. It gave me Cap and a better understanding of why I didn't really fit with Mom, Dad, and Drake. Why Drake hates me."

That hurts my heart. "I don't think he hates you. He's jealous. He has to feel like he's losing everyone now that he knows both of us are Cap's kids. He lost Mom too, then he lost us. We gained a family in Cap. Drake lost everyone but Dad."

"By his own doing," Cam insists.

"Agreed. I have hope for him yet."

"You'll forgive me if I don't hold that same sentiment."

Drake was horrible to Cam. I tried to be an intermediary. Usually, it only redirected their frustration onto me. "You and Drake are like Cap and Dad. The hate will continue if you don't stop the cycle."

"Yes, wise one." He kisses my cheek, making a joke, but he heard me.

Cap steps forward. "Hey, Tay. Do you need anything?"

Cam steps away, giving us a moment.

"I'd like to marry Landry at your house. Nothing big. Just family in your backyard. If that's okay."

His dimpled smile lightens my heart and makes me forget my pain for a minute. "I'd love to throw you a wedding." He glances at Landry. "Have you discussed that with him? I got the impression he doesn't want to wait that long."

"I'll talk to him. I agreed to marry here, but I want Cher and my little brothers and sister there, as well as everyone else in our extended family. He'll understand."

"You give me the okay, and we'll start working on it."

"I have another favor."

"Anything."

"I think I'm going to be laid up for a bit recovering. Do you think we can live with y'all for a while, just till I'm on my feet?" I don't want him to think we'll live there forever.

His swipes at his eyes. "As long as you want, even after you're on your feet. I've got too many years to make up for."

He doesn't have anything to make up for, but I'm glad he doesn't feel like I'm intruding. "Be sure Cher agrees with that. You've got a full house without me and Landry."

"Our house can never be too full, Taylor. Cher and I have already discussed it. We want you and Landry to stay as long as you want." His hold on my hand tightens slightly.

I blink, feeling sleepy all of a sudden. Landry is by my side in the next second, carefully pushing my hair off my forehead, his thumb rubbing back and forth. "You need to sleep." He nods to the white cord with the red button on the end draped across my lap. "Have some pain meds before your pain gets unmanageable."

"Will you stay?" I push the button but need to know I won't be alone.

"Wild horses couldn't drag me away."

"Would you lay with me?"

Cap chuckles. "On that note, I'll get everyone out of here and find us some hotel rooms."

I try to tell him he doesn't need to stay; they should go home. Landry can take care of me. But he's not hearing it. "See you in the morning." He kisses my head and clears the room.

"Now?"

Dually smiles. "There's not enough space in that bed for me too. Plus, you had major surgery. I'll sit in the recliner right next to you and hold your hand. I'm not going anywhere, I promise."

It takes a little begging and tad more pouting, but with the nurse's approval, Landry climbs in bed with me after kicking off his shoes. He glues himself to my right side, my upper body in his embrace, while my left leg remains elevated and untouched. I drift off to sleep with a renewed hope and a deep sense of peace, and some really great drugs coursing through my system.

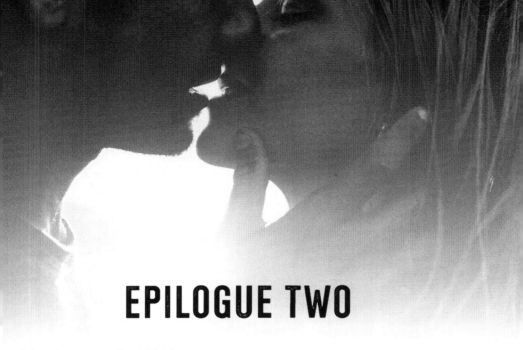

EPILOGUE TWO

TWO WEEKS LATER

"YOU READY FOR THIS?" GABRIEL PATS MY BACK AS I stare at the backyard from the kitchen windows.

"I was made for her." It's that simple and maybe that complicated.

"I know the feeling." His gaze finds Frankie over his shoulder. She stills when she looks up to find his eyes already on her. She blushes and smiles. A silent conversation passes between them.

Love.

I scan the room and find Cap with Cher in his arms, kissing the top of her head, patting her rear, whispering something that makes her laugh and smile at him like he's her everything. Rowdy is only a few feet away with Reese pulled snug in his chest. Their quiet conversation lights up her face, returning his completely-gone-for-her gaze.

Love.

It doesn't hurt to witness anymore.

It isn't a dirty word that only held painful memories, marred by regret and disappointments.

Love.

It's inexhaustible hope.

It's never having to say you're sorry, yet doing it to be sure the other person understands you see them, you hear them, you understand and accept your shortcomings but will strive to do better.

Love is the reason we're here today. The reason I survived my car wreck all those years ago. The reason Taylor survived her attacker—twice. The reason I forgive. The reason I ask and accept her forgiveness.

She is my morning light and my midnight insatiability.

She is my reason.

She is my love.

I swivel in my chair, frowning at my leg splint. "It doesn't do much for the silhouette."

Frankie and Reese share a smile and laugh. "Landry doesn't care what you wear. He's ecstatic you're alive."

Reese moves closer, bending down in her pale blue dress. "He wanted to marry you in the hospital bed right after your surgery."

I smile. "I wanted that too."

"But you were nice enough to wait so we could all be a part of it," Frankie exclaims, rubbing her pregnant belly, ensuring I understand there would have been hell to pay if the women in Landry's life—now mine— would have been left out of our special day. As well as Gabriel and all of the other guys.

"It wouldn't have been about who wasn't there. It was about wanting to commit to each other in a substantial and immediate way to mark the beginning of our second chance." But I totally get where they're coming from. I wouldn't have been happy if Cam had gotten married without me there. I would have tried to understand, but my feelings would have been hurt, and I'd always wish to have been there to witness his joy. I was already feeling insecure about my place in his life since he left Texas. Not being invited to his wedding would have had a deeper meaning close to rejection for me. Probably not for him. It's a matter of perspective.

We each bring our own baggage and selfish needs to the table. They skew our opinions and how we view situations, how we react to others. Hopefully today it's nothing but good stuff all around.

A knock at the door has all eyes turning as Cap pokes his head in. "Are you beautiful ladies ready to get the show on the road?"

Yes! "More than ready." I start to get up, grabbing my crutches. I pray I don't trip or catch the bottom of my dress with them.

Cap grabs my arm, helping me balance. I still can't put any weight on my leg. If the swelling has gone down enough by next week, they'll determine if I need a cast or can continue with the splint or a brace. Thankfully, it's only a hairline tibia fracture.

"I was thinking I might carry you." His dimpled smile is so familiar, like mine and Cam's.

I can't decide if it's sweet or childish to be carried down the aisle by my dad. I'm pretty sure Barrett couldn't do it. I considered walking alone, but I knew it would mean a lot to let my dads do it. "How about you and Barrett push me in my wheelchair?" Then I don't have to mess with my crutches, and they both get to participate.

His smile softens. "It would be my honor."

I look past Cap and see my dad in the doorway. He's been quiet and reserved since I arrived home—Cap's home. Not standoffish, just chill, letting me decide how our relationship moves forward from here. He nods. "I'm just happy to be included, Taylor. Whatever you want that won't cause you pain or discomfort."

"We'll take your crutches in case you need them later." Reese grabs them and heads out with Frankie.

I pivot with Cap's help and sit in the wheelchair I've been using since I came home from the hospital. "Let's do this."

Warmth spreads in my chest as I take in my Songbird, bracketed by her dads pushing her toward me in her wheelchair, her left leg up and visible by the slit in her white pearly dress. This is better than marrying her in her hospital bed and gown. I wouldn't have minded one bit. I think she did. This isn't the big wedding Rowdy said she dreamt of, but it's closer to the one she said she wanted, and I'm all about listening to my girl and what she says and even what she doesn't.

She wanted her family and friends present. She didn't care where or what we wore. But I'm damn sure glad she bought that gorgeous fucking dress.

They make it to me, and before she can say a word, I'm scooping her up into my arms.

"Dually, what are you doing?"

"Getting hitched. What are you doing?" I tease.

Rowdy places a chair behind me, facing sideways with the minister to my right and our friends and family to my left. I sit and gently settle her across my lap, facing the minister, her back to the crowd, but when she locks on me, everyone will see the side of our faces. Rowdy then puts a stool below her left leg to hold it up, not as high as she needs to keep it, but good enough for the short time for us to say *I do*.

She giggles, and my heart soars. "Gettin' married on your lap, apparently."

"That you are. I want you close when we take our vows. I'm not sure I'll ever want to let you go."

She brushes her hand along the side of my face, teasing my hair. "Don't ever let me go."

"Never."

"Ever."

My forehead presses to hers. "Love you, baby."

"Love you right back."

"This is the beginning of our love song."

"I like the sound of that. Can you hum a few lines?" she teases.

"I'd rather get you naked and make your body sing."

A throat clears. We both look to the blushing minister. "Are you ready to begin?"

"We've already started," we say in unison.

"Don't move," he growls, his breath tickling my most intimate parts as he nudges my legs farther apart.

"How can I not move when you're doing that thing with your tongue?" He knows what he's doing. He likes to torture me and then make it seem like I'm misbehaving by moving and begging him for more.

Puh-leeze.

He loves it.

I love it.

"I don't want you to hurt your leg," he mumbles.

Yeah, I don't want to aggravate my leg either. I was aching earlier from standing so much during our after-wedding party. A reception seems too formal for the lowkey event Rowdy and Reese threw for us at his house. We snuck out an hour ago, coming back to Cap's. We considered going to a hotel for a few nights but decided against it. I have too many apparatuses to help me get around and do everyday tasks I took for granted, like taking a shower without the need of a shower chair. Or going to the bathroom and not needing handles to grip and help me get up and down when balancing on one leg. Thus, the toilet rail that fits over the toilet.

It all seems too much to try to live without even for the convenience of total alone time without anyone hearing him pound me into next week. Which he won't be doing because I'm *fragile* and *healing*. I did have a collapsed lung a few weeks ago and bruises all over my face and body that are still mending, not to mention the broken leg.

So, yeah, it's a calmer event. No hanging from chandleries. No wild sex. Just my husband and me making love knowing there's no one else in the house—at least for the next few hours.

I use the term making love lightly because all he's really doing is torturing me, taking me to the edge and bringing me back over and over again.

"I swear to God. If you don't let me come—"

He flicks my clit and silences me with soft sucking and laving, and kneading fingers deep inside, playing me like an instrument he knows so well.

The ringing starts in my ears and spreads like the tingle moving up from my toes.

"That's it, Songbird. Sing for me." His free hand strikes the right note on my breast, squeezing, twisting, flicking.

It's not my singing voice he wants or what he receives, but a guttural moan that comes from deep within, as I'm blinded with lust and the urge to consume him and be consumed. "Landry." I fist his hair.

"Give. It," he growls into me.

Give it.

Give it.

Give it.

I thrust, using my good leg for leverage, lifting into his face, his touch, his magic, wicked fingers.

Ohgodplease!

Yes. Yes. Right there…

I explode. My pleasure feasting on his groans as he eats me like I'm his favorite meal.

I am. I know that much is true.

Panting and quaking, I gasp as he slides into me, rising up and turning me to my side so my bad leg is between his, and my good leg is bent and opening me to his blistering thrusts.

"Fuck, baby." He pistons through each word. "Can't. Get. Deep. Enough." Nipple twist. "You're my wife." His eyes meet mine, and he leans down. "My beautiful, sexy wife."

Damn. My hot, soft-hearted fighter, my soul feeder, my everything rubs my clit, and I squeeze and buck, needing more. Needing *him*.

"Yes, fuck. Just. Like. That." The tips of his fingers rub my clit, circling, circling, circling.

Slick.

Wet.

Heat.

Need.

Fill. Fill. And fill.

One. Joined.

My husband. My heart. My other half.

"Please," I beg, needing to come, *wanting* to come again—with him.

"Almost." He leans forward, letting my leg slip down to his hip, one arm braced beside my head. "I can't believe I get to love you forever, Songbird."

And ever.

And ever.

And ever.

My silent cry brings tears to my eyes as I start to come. He jerks and grinds, growling my name, joining me, filling me, healing me.

Forgiving me.

Loving me.

Completing me.

"Forever," I manage as he kisses me slowly, tenderly, reverently.

"Not done." He pants, nibbling my mouth and sucking my bottom lip.

I smile and grab his face. "You got more, Cowboy?"

His smirk is pure evil. "Planning on riding you till the cows come home, Wife."

Damn, that's going to be a long ride, given we don't have any. I carefully roll to my back and draw him closer with my good leg around his ass. "Give me everything."

He sinks into me, holding his weight. "Everything I have is yours."

"Same. All my good. All my bad."

"I'm a greedy man when it comes to you, Taylor."

"Be greedy." I clench around him, aroused by knowing he wants all of me.

"So fucking greedy, baby."

I dreamt of loving Landry again, of finding a place where we could forgive and move on, but I never thought it would feel this good, this freeing.

He loved me when I was fifteen. Showed me how a man could love a woman, what our future *could* be like.

Now, we're finally ready to live it.

Save a horse, ride a cowboy.

And ride.

And ride.

And ride.

BONUS SCENES

Want more COWBOY and TAYLOR?

Join my mailing list to receive for COWBOY and TAYLOR.
Bonus Scenes are only available for newsletter subscribers.

https://dl.bookfunnel.com/71ggnkfcfz

WHAT'S NEXT?

MUSTANG's story is next.

Add MUSTANG to your TBR.
https://smarturl.it/MUSTANG_TBR

Join my mailing list to stay up to date on MUSTANG's release , other
book news, promotions, and all the happenings.
dmckdavis.com/subscribe

DID YOU ENJOY THIS BOOK?

This is a dream for me to be able to share my love of writing with you.

If you liked my story, please consider leaving a review on Amazon and on Goodreads.

Personal recommendations to your friends and loved ones are a great compliment too. Please share, follow, join my newsletter, and help spread the word—let everyone know how much you loved Landry and Taylor's story.

ACKNOWLEDGMENTS

Thank you to my husband and kids for their endless support and understanding when I'm on deadline and not as available as they or I may like.

Thank you to my author friends and Divas for your camaraderie and support. You feed my soul and lift me up. I am eternally grateful for you.

Thank you to my editors, Tamara and Krista, for helping me get what's in my head on the page, wrangling my dyslexic brain output into grammatically accurate phrasing. You are the icing on my cake.

And to the readers and bloggers, if you're reading this right now, thank you from the bottom of my heart.

Keep reading. I'll keep writing.

I'm blessed to be on this journey. Thank you for taking it with me.
XOXO, Dana

ABOUT THE AUTHOR

D.M. Davis is a Contemporary and New Adult Romance Author.

She is a Texas native, wife, and mother. Her background is Project Management, technical writing, and application development. D.M. has been a lifelong reader and wrote poetry in her early life, but has found her true passion in writing about love and the intricate relationships between men and women.

She writes of broken hearts and second chances, of dreamers looking for more than they have and daring to reach for it.

D.M. believes it is never too late to make a change in your own life, to become the person you always wanted to be, but were afraid you were not worth the effort.

You are worth it. Take a chance on you. You never know what's possible if you don't try. Believe in yourself as you believe in others, and see what life has to offer.

Please visit her website, dmckdavis.com, for more details, and keep in touch by signing up for her newsletter, and joining her on Facebook, Reader Group, Instagram, Twitter, and TikTok.

ADDITIONAL BOOKS BY
D.M. DAVIS

UNTIL YOU SERIES
Book 1 – Until You Set Me Free
Book 2 – Until You Are Mine
Book 3 – Until You Say I Do
Book 3.5 – Until You eBook Boxset
Book 4 – Until You Believe
Book 5 – Until You Forgive
Book 6 – Until You Save Me

FINDING GRACE SERIES
Book 1 – The Road to Redemption

BLACK OPS MMA SERIES
Book 1 – No Mercy
Book 2 – Rowdy
Book 3 – Captain
Book 4 – Cowboy
Book 5 – Mustang

WILD DUET
Book 1 – WILDFLOWER (in Heroes with Heat
and Heart 2 charity anthology)
Book 2 – WILDFIRE

STANDALONES
Warm Me Softly
Doctor Heartbreak

https://dmckdavis.com/

JOIN MY READER GROUP

www.facebook.com/groups/dmdavisreadergroup

STALK ME

Visit www.dmckdavis.com for more details about my books.
Keep in touch by signing up for my Newsletter.
Connect on social media: Reader's Group, Facebook, Instagram,
Twitter, Tiktok
Follow me: BookBub, Goodreads, Amazon

Printed in Great Britain
by Amazon

30633239R00135